His Australian
Heiress

By Margaret Way

Her Australian Hero
His Australian Heiress

Available from Lyrical Books

And coming from Zebra Books
in November:
Poinciana Road

Published by Kensington Publishing Corporation

His Australian Heiress

Margaret Way

LYRICAL SHINE
Kensington Publishing Corp.
www.kensingtonbooks.com

LYRICAL SHINE BOOKS are published by

Kensington Publishing Corp.
119 West 40th Street
New York, NY 10018

All Kensington titles, imprints, and distributed lines are available at special quantity discounts for bulk purchases for sales promotion, premiums, fund-raising, educational, or institutional use.

Special book excerpts or customized printings can also be created to fit specific needs. For details, write or phone the office of the Kensington Sales Manager: Kensington Publishing Corp., 119 West 40th Street, New York, NY 10018. Attn. Sales Department. Phone: 1-800-221-2647.

Lyrical Shine and Lyrical Shine logo Reg. U.S. Pat. & TM Off.

First Electronic Edition: September 2016
eISBN-13: 978-1-60183-766-0
eISBN-10: 1-60183-766-6

First Print Edition: September 2016
ISBN-13: 978-1-60183-767-7
ISBN-10: 1-60183-767-4

Printed in the United States of America

To my good friend and fellow traveller in our long writing careers, Helen Bianchin.

Chapter 1

The distinguished principal of Asherton School for Girls, Dr. Vivienne Granger herself, came to the door of the Great Hall to deliver an urgent message to one of her students. For the Head to do such a thing was unheard of. There were lesser mortals to whom she could delegate such tasks, but this was a very serious matter. It needed discretion from the very top, and no one topped the benevolent, on occasion fearsome, Dr. Vivienne Granger.

A rehearsal of *The Merchant of Venice* was in progress. Charlotte Mansfield, Head Girl, handpicked by Dr. Granger on merit, not on her illustrious name, was halfway into Portia's famous speech, "The quality of mercy is not strained." Charlotte had reached, "Wherein doth sit the dread and fear of kings . . . ," making a brilliant job of it according to the college's speech and drama teacher, Dr. Phillipa Redding, when Dr. Granger lifted a long, black-clad arm and began waggling imperious fingers in Charlotte's direction. It was a clear indication Charlotte was to break off and join her.

Just wait for what's coming.

The message popped instantly into Charlotte's head. It came from someone, maybe God, but she had no clear belief that was so. She had given up wondering where her sixth sense came from. Perhaps everyone was born with such a sense but made the decision not to cultivate it because it made them nervous. And rightly so. It was scary. The message she received was crystal clear and unequivocal.

Your grandfather is dead.

She felt the flow of blood in her veins turn to ice. For the past five years as a boarder at Asherton, life had grown quiet around her. Quiet, even pleasantly serene. The terrible grief, the sense of loss, the melancholy, had gradually given way to her natural urge to live her

2 • *Margaret Way*

life, to succeed. She was a Mansfield. Success was expected of her. Mansfields were very serious folk. Under the leadership of her grandfather, real results in life were expected to be achieved, even if one was told at age twelve one's parents had been killed.

"All eyes will be on you now, Charlie. Survive this, my girl, and you're made. I know you have it in you. You've inherited a good dollop of me."

Charlotte already knew about that dollop, but *made*? What sort of a promise was that? How conducive to a peaceful life? She remembered her darling father once saying some days it was all he could do to get out of bed. She had adored her father. Her beautiful mother, Alyssa, too, but her mother had not brought good news to the family.

"Charlotte, dear, fix your hair." Dr. Granger's voice brought her out of her sad reverie. Dr. Granger was determined for Charlotte to look well cared for, even cherished, which she had been. Everyone in the school, even the inclined-to-be-nasty girls, something she as Head Girl had worked hard to stamp out of them, had rallied around the twelve-year-old Charlotte Mansfield, who had lost both mother and father in a horrific car crash. It had occurred while Charlotte's father, Christopher Mansfield, accompanied by his beautiful society wife, was driving down a steep incline not far from the Mansfields' magnificent country house, Clouds, in the Blue Mountains. There had been a lot of gossip at the time that the couple could well have been arguing. The marriage, according to a "close friend," who remained steadfastly nameless and faceless, had been a "bumpy ride." The bumpy ride had come to a tragic dead end.

There was a long, long waiting list for would-be pupils to get into Asherton. Many were entered at birth. Even Dr. Granger couldn't keep track of the numbers. Charlotte, who had never had a female relative so she had no role model, as a pupil of the school had arrived in a chauffeur-driven Rolls. It had been reported like something out of the movies, which in many ways it had been. The girl's beauty, her manner, her clothes, the aura she gave off of being looked after by a whole team of uniformed servants, set onlookers agog. Since that advantageous day, Mansfield money kept the ball rolling for Asherton. Mansfield largesse had provided many of the splendid amenities, including the total overhauling and cataloguing of their fine library.

"If you'd just tell me, Dr. Granger," Charlotte now said in a perfectly courteous voice, making short work of turning her long, riotously curly blond hair into an elegant knot.

"Mr. Macmillan, *young* Mr. Macmillan that is, will tell you all you need to know, Charlotte," said Dr. Granger.

"Someone up there was already determined to beat him to it," Charlotte spoke in her disconcertingly adult way. "My grandfather is dead."

Dr. Granger, who had started to shake her head, stopped. "My dear, young Mr. Macmillan is here. He's waiting for you in the Visitors' Room. Tea and coffee have been arranged."

"Thank you, ma'am," Charlotte returned gravely.

Charlotte always managed to make her feel like royalty, Dr. Granger thought with a surge of gratification. "I'm here for you, Charlotte," she said, with genuine concern. She well-remembered the bereft child Charlotte Mansfield had been, packed off to boarding school at age twelve. Dr. Granger had the greatest respect and affection for her student. Charlotte was a survivor. On the other hand, she would have been hard-pressed to find a kind word for Sir Reginald Mansfield, co-founder of the blue chip law firm Mansfield-Macmillan. However brilliant Sir Reginald had been, he was a tyrant of a man with a tongue that lashed out at just about everyone in sight. Indeed, there had been a positive scarcity of people, her included, who had had the temerity to stand up to him and his glacier-green eyes. There was even the rumour his insiders called him Attila the Hun.

The upside, however, was that Sir Reginald had earned a well-deserved reputation not only as a brilliant legal mind, but as one of the country's outstanding philanthropists. Now that his life was done, Dr. Granger had the un-Christian-like thought, the devil might well lead Sir Reginald on his merry way. Possibly in handcuffs.

The Visitors' Room, where parents of boarders took tea, coffee, and conversation with their female offspring, was a large, beautiful, welcoming room, with first-class furnishings, prized paintings by leading Australian artists—two of whom had their names on Asherton's Honour Board—dove-grey velvet upholstered sofas on opposite sides of a venerable Chinese chest that served as a coffee table, the light coming from a pair of tall leaded windows. At that time in the afternoon, sunshine was streaming a rainbow gold into the room.

Brendon Macmillan, grandson of Sir Hugo Macmillan, had been

4 · *Margaret Way*

looking out of the graceful arched windows at the splendid school grounds. He turned at their approach. His eyes fell immediately on Charlotte in her truly dreary school uniform: white blouse, green tie, and green checked skirt worn to the knee. Somehow Charlotte made that impossible outfit look almost smart. One either had style or one didn't. He stood a moment longer, taking in her body language and her expression, which actually gave nothing away. Charlotte was a Mansfield. He could never forget that, but she was far and away the pick of the bunch.

"I've brought Charlotte, as you can see, Mr. Macmillan," Dr Granger said in her cultured contralto. "Afternoon tea will be served in fifteen minutes."

"How kind of you, Dr. Granger." Brendon executed a suave bow. It was a gesture that came naturally to him; consequently it was utterly charming. So much so, the single Dr. Granger pinked and then withdrew with a smile that made her look ten years younger.

"So they sent you, Bren, to tell me," Charlotte said by way of greeting. "That's a relief."

"You've guessed, or rather intuited?" Of course she knew. Charlotte Mansfield was an uncanny young creature. He gestured towards a sofa, waiting for her to be seated before taking the one opposite.

"Too much for you to accept female intuition illuminates?" she asked, large emerald-green eyes glittering like jewels in a clear, un-made-up face. Not that it mattered. Charlotte had no need of artifice. It was almost with a sense of shock that he realized Charlotte was on the cusp of turning into a beautiful, strong, and charismatic woman.

"Not with you, Charlie," he said dryly.

"Besides, it's not as though I get many visitors," she added, on a fine caustic note. She did sarcasm well. "Apart from you and your welcome visits, the rest of you decided to leave me in peace."

It was so true, he felt a pang of regret and genuine empathy. "You've made a damned good job hacking it alone," he said. Charlotte, though she had had every right to be, had never become an overemotional, extremely needy child. He admired that immensely.

"Well, it's not as though I give a blankety-blank for anyone anyway," she replied coolly. "Apart from Poppa, who hadn't planned on dying, and you, I've been all too easy to ignore."

He laughed despite himself. "Calling your grandfather 'Poppa' is as incongruous as calling the pope 'Frank.'"

"Poppa dearly loved me, hard as it is to believe. We didn't wear our hearts on our sleeves. Poppa told me if I survived the deaths of my parents I'd be made. I guess as I'm doing well here, I must be, don't you think?"

"You're a bit of a phenomenon all on your own, Charlie," he said. "You're beautiful, or you will be when you can shake off that dreadful uniform. You're clever, and, I have to concede, a chip or two off the old block."

"Okay, or not okay," she said. "I'm going to take that as a compliment anyway. I'm tough, Bren. I'm glad you've accepted that. It might make life easier for both of us now that my whole life is about to change. No matter what the public thinks happens behind the scenes, the Mansfields and the Macmillans hate one another's guts."

"Charlotte, Charlotte," he sighed.

She cut him off with a swish of her hand. "Please . . . don't bother to deny it."

A shadow crossed his handsome face. "There are reasons."

"So you have access to truths I don't have?" she challenged. "Or are they secrets? I have heard just about all of the ugly rumours."

His lips tightened. "Are you talking about your parents' marriage or what?"

"Rumours became part of my everyday life, Bren. Think about that. Part of your life, too?"

"As far as I'm concerned, the rumours about your mother and my father are unspeakable," he said grimly.

"They're *spoken*, regardless, Bren," she pointed out. "One part of me wants to know everything about it. Another part warns me to leave well enough alone. Let it lie. No wonder your mother hates me."

He didn't answer for a while. "Charlie, my mother doesn't hate you at all," he said in a perturbed voice. "No one does. You've been the victim in this. The trauma went back much further to our grandfathers. My grandfather was never as ruthless as yours, not that I wish to speak ill of the dead."

"So you're toning it down? You think now there's a possibility I might join forces with the enemy now that my grandfather is gone? He has gone, hasn't he? Am I right?" she asked, fixing him with her beautiful, highly intelligent eyes.

He nodded. "Of course you're right. I knew the moment I laid eyes on you, you knew why I'm here. Forget my family for a moment."

"How can I? It's not just you and me, Bren. It's me and them. All families are mysterious. Ours are more mysterious than most. More money. More betrayals. More secrets, most of them hidden. You're asking me to forget the unhappiness of it all. The troubling thing is that unhappiness vibrates in the memory." She paused for a moment, and then suddenly revealed, "I have memories that flash in and out of my consciousness. I can't snatch them back. Repressed memories. Floods of feelings I've had to lock away so they've become as good as inaccessible."

"That's your survival mechanism, Charlie," he said, understanding perfectly. He had his own set of repressed memories.

"Yours, too, I bet," Charlotte said, confirming her sharp intuitions.

"Don't *I* get any credit at all for being your friend?"

"Well . . . I agree that our friendship is too important to mess with," she said, as though the thought had just struck her. "You've been the light at the end of the dark tunnel. You've always been kind to me, despite your full program and all your lady friends. What are you, again? Australia's most eligible bachelor?"

Irritation engulfed him. "Charlie, don't bother me with that idiotic guff. Not my idea at all. I pray for a quiet life. I can't help what labels the media stick on me."

"Bren, you're a dream!" Charlotte threw back her head theatrically, closing her eyes. "You even on occasion behave like one."

"Thanks a lot."

"The thinking woman's fantasy," she continued.

"I told you to stop," Brendon said, warningly.

"And so I shall." She didn't want Bren to go away. "It's payback, I guess. I haven't seen much of you lately."

His handsome mouth compressed. "Which would indicate I've been extremely busy."

"Of course."

In his midtwenties, Brendon Macmillan was tall, rangy, more handsome than any man had need to be. He had also earned the reputation for having a splendid mind. She had known Bren all her life. She had grown up with his treating her as his young cousin. He was infinitely kinder than the rest of the Macmillans. A cold-blooded lot, she had always thought. It wasn't an overstatement. It was a description that matched them perfectly. Except Bren.

"I'm here to keep you on track, Bren," she said.

"You do a good job of it, too, but this is a very serious occasion. We wanted you to know before the story breaks. You can bet it will be today."

"How thoughtful of your family to send *you*." She took a quick mock glance at her watch. "What time do they want you back?"

He took a moment to chill out. "Sir Reginald had a major heart attack around eleven a.m. this morning. My grandfather was actually at Clouds at the time. It was thought Sir Reginald might pull through. He was certainly fighting to stay alive, but he refused point-blank to go to hospital. No one had the guts to ignore him and call for an ambulance."

"If he had to die, he wanted to die at Clouds," Charlotte said simply. "His number was up."

"He was truly a most remarkable man," Brendon said, despite the fact that Sir Reginald had been crowned a tyrant.

"You Macmillans will be hoping you won't see his like again," Charlotte spoke with adult asperity.

He couldn't let that slide. "*Two* Sir Reginalds would be far too stressful," Brendon said. "Anyway, I'm sure we won't. Sir Reginald was a monumental man, but he hurt people one way or another. He hurt *my* people."

"The odd thing is, he liked *you,* Bren."

Brendon considered that. "I have to admit, he was relatively mellow when I was around."

"He said that if he were a lion, you were a black panther. He told me that the last time I saw him, which was about two months ago. He also told me I had to watch out for you."

He gave her a searching look out of his silver-grey eyes. "Do I remind you of a black panther, fanciful as it sounds?"

Charlotte canted her head to one side. "There *is* a quality, but ask me again when you're forty. In the meantime, I'll be keeping a close watch on you. My father could have made a good job of filling Poppa's shoes. He was clever, but much gentler, thank the Lord, with far more understanding. Artistic, too. My dear uncle Conrad, who has managed to forget I even exist, couldn't possibly have stepped into Poppa's shoes. Uncle Conrad, now a famous author, though he's a mite slow coming up with another blockbuster, I notice." She paused for a moment, as though she was trying to settle something in her mind. "Oddly enough, it was my father who was the compulsive writer, recorder, whatever. He always had a notebook handy, jotting things down. I do it myself. Phrases I think need to be captured. Certain words. Lovely words that stimulate the imagination. I love language. I'm the class freak that way."

"I don't know about freak," he said dryly, well aware of Charlotte's abilities. "Top of the class, straight A student. Your uncle Conrad has been swanning around the country house for years now." He didn't bother to hide his distaste. Conrad Mansfield, in his opinion, was a self-important, callous man. One didn't expect a fine writer to be cruel. On the contrary, a writer would need to be a person of compassion.

"Maybe he needed some encouragement from Poppa, who despised him," Charlotte said by way of explanation. "You don't happen to know the reason, do you?" She shot him a keen glance.

Brendon tried to give her at least part of the truth. "I think Sir Reginald found it painful that your uncle bounced back so quickly after his brother's tragic death. It's no secret Conrad had a lifelong problem with sibling jealousy."

"I expect it was hard for him, with my father being Poppa's clear favourite and heir." Charlotte always tried to be fair. "Anyway, Uncle Conrad has made a name for himself in literary circles. Personally I didn't think he had a book in him, let alone what is considered a minor masterpiece."

"You've read it?" Brendon raised an enquiring black brow.

"Of course I've read it, Bren," she said, tartly. "Don't be ridiculous. Have you?"

"Like you, I didn't think he had it in him." Brendon shrugged. "They're talking about making it into a film. I believe Cate Blanchett has been approached."

"Really? She would be perfect as Laura," Charlotte said. "This is a strange conversation, isn't it?"

"All our conversations are strange, Charlie." There was an enigmatic look in his luminous eyes, made more startling in contrast to his bronzed skin and his jet-black hair and brows. "Are you sad?" he asked, unsure what was going on behind her small, composed face.

She shook her head slowly. "I wouldn't term it like that, Bren. Poppa was a very *distant* figure, with a whole side of his life not accessible to me. At the time of my parents' death, I was still a child, remember."

"A highly intelligent, thinking twelve-year-old landed with as much grief as any child could bear. I remember how observant you were even then. Observant well beyond your years."

Charlotte's slender shoulders rose and fell. "More's the pity! I'd have done better not to have been so watchful. I've hardly seen Poppa in the past five years. I really have no reason to *love* him, except I do. *Did.* As my *grandfather,* which is not to say I *liked* him. I think his only friend was your grandfather, and even he had to walk away. Poppa was into his eighties, not that he looked anything like it or acted anything like it. He *hated* growing older, losing his physical powers."

"He didn't see it coming, Charlie."

"None of us see it coming unless we hold a gun to our heads, like that poor stockbroker in the papers. I'm sorry if I appear too calm."

"I didn't expect floods of tears, Charlotte," he said. "You've had a lot to bear."

She brought up her blond head. Golden tendrils were curling onto her forehead and the sides of her cheeks, increasing her angelic look. However, Charlie had access to a keen tongue that took people aback. "I wasn't going to set myself up for more pain, Bren," she explained. "I was in tatters after my parents were killed. I adored my father. I loved my mother, too, though I didn't see a lot of her. She liked to escape. Besides, she had functions to go to from daylight to dark. My father was always there for me. Even Poppa was different when my father was alive. When my father was killed, whatever Poppa had used for a heart got shoved into a steel box. A little heart he kept back for me. I was Christopher's child, the same blond hair and green eyes. Poppa's green eyes. Poppa made your family pay for your part in my father's death."

Brendon's arresting features became a taut mask. "He made my family pay far too much for far too long."

"The Mansfields and the Macmillans have a terrible history," she said. "It's hate that links us far more than friendship."

"Isn't it up to us, Charlie, not to let it go on a moment longer?"

Brendon implored. "Despite everything, our grandfathers stuck together as partners. They were together at the end. My grandfather is not a rogue."

"Leastways, not that we know." She emphasized the "*know.*"

He ignored that, continuing on. "One reason Sir Reginald trusted him."

"I believe he did," Charlotte had to concede. "I expect, too, that Sir Hugo had a great deal on Poppa. If my grandfather had a weakness, Sir Hugo was the only one to know it. And he didn't breathe a word about it. Admirable, in its way."

Brendon stared back at her. Charlotte Mansfield, at seventeen, was far more intelligent and more knowledgeable on a whole variety of subjects, including human psychology, than any other young woman he knew.

"The funeral?" she suddenly asked with a frown. "No state funeral. That's out of the question."

The tone was worthy of Sir Reginald. "Atta girl! That's the spirit." The old devil didn't deserve a state funeral.

"No spirit involved," Charlotte said. She was more aware than Brendon that her grandfather had been no saint.

"There's only one hitch, Charlie. There's your uncle Conrad," he reminded her.

"Never mind Uncle Conrad," Charlotte replied with an oddly familiar sweep of her hand. "No state funeral. We can't avoid a large funeral."

"No," he agreed. The legal community, the business community, the Establishment, anyone who was anyone, would make it their business to attend and be photographed doing it.

"I'll be there, for Poppa," Charlotte said. "I will speak for him. He will come over as a loving father and grandfather. We can't allow his terrifying persona to get in the way. I'll need clothes. My friend Natalie's mother will help me choose."

"That's Marella Hatton?" he asked. Charlotte would be in safe hands with Marella, who consistently won the vote for best dressed.

Charlotte nodded. "She's a lovely woman, so kind, so elegant. I can't let Poppa down."

"You won't, Charlotte," Brendon said with absolute certainty.

She smiled at him, with very nearly a tear glistening. "You're my man, Bren!"

"I try to be," he said wryly, knowing full well it was going to turn out to be a very difficult role.

So, at seventeen years of age, Charlotte Mansfield became Sir Reginald Mansfield's heiress, the primary beneficiary of his will, ahead of a long list of expected beneficiaries, institutions, charities, and the like. Charlotte had taken precedence over Sir Reginald's remaining son, Conrad, who nevertheless had been amply provided for, as was Conrad's son, Simon, his only child.

The reading of the will, however, remained in everyone's memory as a horror session. Conrad Mansfield had afterwards taken expert legal advice to contest the will, but all efforts had come to nothing. Sir Reginald had seen to that. Conrad Mansfield had been left a rich man. He was no longer a partner in Mansfield-Macmillan after all. He was an author with, in most people's opinion, a dream of a life.

If he had ignored his niece for much of her life, his hostility and resentment burned ever brighter as his teenage niece grew into womanhood. His resentment surprised no one, least of all Charlotte. Conrad Mansfield had not been appointed her guardian until she attained her majority. That role had fallen to Sir Hugo Macmillan. Sir Hugo had been handed considerable responsibility, which he took very seriously. Charlotte Mansfield had been brought up understanding the concept of power. It was in the blood.

Chapter 2

Four years later...

Charlotte took the elevator to the top floor of the Mansfield Building with rippling waves running through her. She exited the lift
and then walked down the carpeted corridor to Brendon's office,
giving the very pretty young woman at a front desk, bearing the
name tag, Rebecca, a wave. Rebecca waved back. A moment later,
she knocked on the door with Bren's name on it and then opened it.

"Got a minute?" she asked, walking in regardless.

"Hit me," Brendon said, humour in his silver-grey eyes. He was
slouching back elegantly in his chrome and leather chair, two hands
behind his handsome dark head.

"I won't hold you up. I know how busy you are, even if you don't
look it."

"You can always come back later," he said, slowly straighten-
ing up.

"Oh, sorry, sorry, sorry. My lord." Charlotte threw back her mane
of golden hair. It waved deeply to her shoulders, where it flipped out
in foaming curls. "I'll only take five minutes of your precious time."

"No need to call me 'my lord,' Charlie. At least not yet."

"You sure you want to be a judge?" she asked, studying him
closely. No wonder so many women got carried away by Bren. He
was an extraordinarily attractive man, sophisticated and sexy, the
sort of man women hankered after and longed to meet. For all that,
he didn't have a conceited bone in his body, which was more than
she could say for most males of her acquaintance.

"My vocation, Charlie," he said. "You look great, by the way."
He looked her over with an approving smile. At almost twenty-one,

it was hard to take one's eyes off of Charlotte Mansfield, the heiress. Apart from her beauty, her dress code made everyone sit up and pay attention. Her bronze leather jacket spoke top Italian design, as did her custom-made jeans. Underneath she wore a collarless white silk shirt. All garments worn with flair. Wedge-heeled boots gave her five-three an extra few inches. An expensive-looking leather tote bag was slung carelessly over one shoulder.

Charlotte took a chair opposite him. "How kind of you to say so, Brendon dear."

"Well, you certainly don't need Marella these days."

"Of course I need her," Charlotte said loyally. "She's my honorary aunt. I'll never look as good as Marella."

"You're already there, sweetie pie," he assured her. "So, let's get down to business. I've a cold case I'm working on."

He had her full attention. She was, after all, in her final year of reading Law. "Interesting?" she asked.

"The unsolved murder of Zara Goldberg," he said.

"Before my time."

"Nineteen ninety."

"Ah, yes!" Charlotte cried. "I remember now. Wasn't it thought it was the second husband or the stepson? Or both? She was extremely rich."

Brendon nodded. "From an old Jewish family resettled in Australia. His wife gave the stepson an alibi. The husband was at his club. Both had developed an insatiable taste for money. Madame Goldberg had forked out plenty, and then she stopped, telling hubby and playboy stepson there was no more. It's been a lot of work trying to draw all the pieces together," he said, running a taut hand through his crow-black hair. "I can't afford to make any mistakes."

"Your father is handling the case?"

"Of course."

"Only you're doing all the work," she said breezily.

"Be *pleased* for me, Charlie," he begged. "I know I'm a big help to Dad. But he's the hugely experienced QC at the top of his game. I'm only on my way."

"I *am* pleased for you, Bren," she stressed. "Better yet, I'm proud of you. You just happen to be my favourite Macmillan."

"What can I say to that"—he shrugged—"when you think ill of everyone else?"

"Not *ill*, precisely," she qualified. "It's all a matter of trust. We've learned to tolerate one another these past few years, though your mother will never get around to hugging me."

"Not when you clearly don't want to be hugged," Brendon didn't hesitate to point out.

"True. I might have welcomed a hug as a child, but never mind. Sir Hugo is a man of conscience. He's done his very best for me. Now it's all coming to an end. In another month I'll turn twenty-one."

"And that's a good feeling?" he asked.

Her beautiful green eyes sparkled with satisfaction. "You bet. It's time I began to exercise my powers."

Brendon stared across the desk at her. "What is it you want to change, Charlie?" he asked, very seriously indeed. He had grown very protective of Charlie, only the more protective, the more the worry. Charlotte Mansfield wasn't an amenable young woman. She ruffled sedate feathers. Many people, including his own family members, had been far too slow to take Charlie's measure. His own grandfather was of the belief that young women were to be seen and enjoyed but not heard. Old-school stuff he didn't go along with. Charlotte was already making her mark.

Charlotte didn't have to think for one second. "My grandfather, for all his lack of tolerance for others in his circle, was a genuine philanthropist. I want to step up programs that have fallen into a certain decline, or perhaps handled with too much caution. I want to get more involved in the culture of the city. The Arts is one area crying out for more funding."

"You can do all that," Brendon said, his expression signifying his approval. "You don't have to pitch headlong into it, though. Everything you want to do needs serious discussion." He and Charlotte had had many long conversations over the years when she endeavoured to outline her hopes and plans. Coming into a considerable fortune brought great responsibilities to the right-minded.

"No point in inheriting a great deal of money if one doesn't do worthwhile things with it," Charlotte pointed out, not for the first time. "An area of great moment to me is violence against women. We've spoken about it lots of times before. I want to buy the old Toohey Building. I see it's come on the market. Renovate it. Offer it as a shelter for women and children who are victims of domestic violence."

"As far as I know, Charlotte, the building is all but falling down," Brendon said, a vertical frown between his black brows.

"Then we pull it down. Rebuild. I won't be thwarted."

"There will be a few people not overly fond of your plans," Brendon warned her. He knew of a shady developer or two who were planning on securing the old building.

"We'll face that when we come to it," she said with characteristic self-confidence.

"Who is *we* exactly?" Brendon asked, lifting his brows.

She gave him a lovely smile. "You and me, pal. I want *you,* not your grandfather or your father, looking after my affairs, Bren. I plan on appointing you my advisor. You're not working on full throttle yet, but you soon will be. You're spoken of very highly by the big guns. Professor Morgenstern never lets up singing your praises."

"The Prof is a great friend of my dad's," Brendon pointed out.

"Your dad is not a great friend of mine. As I've said a million and one times, you're the only Macmillan I trust."

He gave her a tight smile. "My dad doesn't deserve your mistrust, Charlie."

"I understand perfectly. You're biased," she said, staring back at him.

"I can live with that. I love my dad."

"I didn't say you were perfect." Charlotte wondered if Brendon's father, Julian, ever thought of her dead mother. Did their affair *really* happen? Or had the rumours sprung from malice? Surely many lives had been ruined by lies. She physically pulled back as a tiny chink of memory opened up in her head.

"Think whatever you like, Christopher. I thought there was trust between us. It seems not. Keep up the accusations and I'll move out. I'll take Charlie."

"What is it?" Brendon leaned forward, a note of urgency in his voice.

She shook her head as if to clear it. "Nothing."

"It had to be something," Bren insisted. "You turned inwards. You looked like you had remembered something?"

She felt his penetrating regard. "Just a flash, Bren. My mother was saying she was moving out and taking me. My father must have been accusing her of something, something she vigorously denied."

"The destructive rumours?" he suggested.

"I expect you're right." She had great faith in Brendon and his high intelligence. At twenty-nine Bren was still a junior barrister, but no one doubted, least of all Charlotte, that he would in a few years take silk, which meant becoming a Queen's Counsel. He would then be following in the steps of his father and grandfather. Sir Hugo was still nominal Head of Chambers, but Brendon's father, Julian Macmillan, was the preeminent senior counsel. Charlotte was in her final year at law school, where she had gained a stand-out reputation as an extremely bright, hardworking student, with the promise of a brilliant future ahead of her.

What Charlotte wanted above all was to follow Brendon's footsteps into criminal law. Her interest was defence, whereas Brendon had already successfully prosecuted minor league criminal cases. Serious criminal matters for both private and legal aid clients were naturally referred to one or other of the seven members of Chambers, all silks.

"So, what's this, then, a day off?" he asked, dropping the subject as Charlie had gone a little pale. He'd seen her maybe four or five times in the past work-filled month.

"I called in sick," she said, breezily. "Not true. Tough class this morning. I wanted to ask you if you'd come with me this weekend to Clouds. You can bring a girlfriend if you like. Lovely Lisa Dixon, isn't it?"

Brendon made a little movement of impatience. "As heartbreaking as it is, Lisa and I broke up. I don't think Lisa wants me back."

"Not what I heard." Charlotte's response was swift and tart.

"Weren't you just the teeniest-weeniest bit jealous?" He gave her one of his heart-stopping smiles. He had beautiful white teeth that heightened the effect of that smile, especially set against his yearlong tan. Bren and his sailing pals were always out on the Harbour on his yacht, *Wild Rose*. He had told her once he had named it after her. Brendon didn't lie. She had no reason to doubt it.

"Jealous? So you noticed?" she joked. "Actually, I quite like Lovely Lisa. At least she's got a brain. Why is it you blokes are so intimidated by brainy women?"

"What, *me*?" he asked in a pseudo-shocked tone.

"I long to say no, but I well remember the long line of beauty queens over the past few years. Is it sex? Is that the whole of it, Bren?" she asked, quite seriously. "I really want to know. Most of my girlfriends have lost sight of chastity, if they've even heard of it at all. Casual sex, to my mind, is courting disaster. Besides, just how many people does one meet that one is physically attracted to? So, sex, what next? Is it a case of 'been there, done that, move on'? Is it the chase, Bren?"

"As if I'm going to discuss this with you now, Charlie," he said. "It will have to be another time. Though I have to tell you, my ex-girlfriends all remain my friends."

She gave a brisk nod. "See what good manners will do? But I still don't get it." She shook her curling mane that was fashionably tamed. "Sex sure isn't on my mind."

"I'm very glad to hear it," Brendon returned with mock gravity. "We're all expecting you to concentrate on topping your final year. Graduate with honours."

"Like you, and to the chagrin of my male colleagues, my career comes first."

"Exactly." He nodded his approval. The thought of Charlie having sex with any of her admirers filled him with something approaching horror. If he knew of any guy in particular, he'd soon tell them to cool it. His outlook, he realized, was almost medieval. "You're about to turn twenty-one," he said, adopting a high moral tone. "You'll be pursued by fortune hunters, though the word is that you've been hotly pursued right through University, right?"

"No one has touched my heart, Bren. If I did have such an admirer, I suspect you'd grab the guy and warn him off. So, you'll come on your own?" she asked.

"Did I say I *would* come?" he taunted, giving her a half smile.

"I know you will. That's how it works. You look out for me."

"So, what are we going *for*? Last time out, I thought Uncle Conrad's spectacular change of heart was entirely bogus."

"It is. After all, I'm allowing him to stay at Clouds."

"So you're set on having your twenty-first at the house, then? Not a hotel?"

"The house," she confirmed. "The only happy times of my early life were spent at Clouds. I don't want a big party. Hundreds of people all swanning about. No more than forty or fifty. There are eight bedrooms at the house. The guest annex will take six to eight. The rest can be put up at Blue Horizons. I've already spoken to Ewan Craig, the proprietor."

"So you've thought it all through. Why then are we going to the house for the weekend, may I ask?"

"It's a wonder you haven't guessed. The only people who aren't aware of my plans are Uncle Conrad and darling Aunt Patricia," she explained. "If I give them enough notice, they might take off for the Maldives or go visit my charming cousin, Simon, in New York."

"No wonder they didn't try again after Simon," Brendon said acidly. The Simon Mansfield he had known had lived life as an incredible snob. The exalted son of an exalted family. Simon had come home for his grandfather's funeral. He had attended reading of the will with his parents, clearly expecting to be a major benefactor. In no way had he been comforted by a couple of million to help him on his career path, with maybe a top American venture capital firm. He had thrown down the gauntlet, standing up astonished, to shout at Charlotte that no way was she going to be allowed to control the Mansfield fortune. His outrage had been matched by that of his doting mother. Conrad Mansfield had kept his outrage on a relatively tight leash.

"Perhaps he's been reborn?" Charlotte suggested. "According to Aunt Patricia, he's doing wonderfully well."

"I'd take that with a grain of salt," Brendon said dryly. "I for one don't believe it for a second. As for your aunt and uncle, everyone has expected them to split for years now."

"Not darling Aunt Pat," Charlotte said. "She'd lose access to wads and wads of money."

Brendon glanced down at the pile of documents on his desk. "So what time do you want to leave?" he asked. Truth was, he felt in need of Charlie's bracing company. She was like a gust of fresh air sweeping through a stuffy room.

"Around eight o'clock Saturday morning," she said. "Suit you? I'll drive."

His silver-grey eyes glittered. "I'm going to refuse your offer right there, babe."

"Spoilsport! I'm every bit as good a driver as you," she claimed.

"Sorry, you're not," he answered emphatically. "You took ages to learn Reverse Park."

"Hey, it wasn't that bad. You used to make me nervous. It's not as though we're going to reverse up the mountain. Okay, then, *you* drive. Not that I've ever had the pleasure of driving your beloved

Aston Martin." The iconic car had been a twenty-first birthday present to Brendon from his father, another vintage car enthusiast.

"I'll let you when I think you can treat it with respect," he said, his glittery gaze on her.

"When will that be?"

Brendon stood up. "Let's keep it this way for now, shall we? What about a bite of lunch? I'm starving."

Charlotte, too, stood up, hoisting her mustard-coloured bag onto her shoulder. "I thought you'd never ask."

The Mansfield country house, Clouds, was a ninety-minute drive from Sydney. It was situated in the beautiful Blue Mountains, a mountainous region of the state of New South Wales, renowned for its spectacular scenery and its forests of oil-bearing eucalyptus trees. It had been thought for years that the blue haze that gave the region its name was caused by the droplets of eucalyptus oil in the atmosphere, but science had identified the magical blue haze as a phenomena common to mountainous regions in other parts of the world. Whatever the answer, and many still held to the eucalyptus oil droplets, thousands of tourists took a trip there each year. All without exception wanted to see and photograph the famous rock formations, the Three Sisters: Meehni, Wimiah, and Gunneddoo. According to aboriginal legend, all three sisters had unwisely fallen in love with men of a different tribe. To protect them from certain death as a tribal war began, a powerful witch doctor had turned them into stone for eternity. It was a good story and a brilliant sight. All three sisters stood three thousand feet tall, towering over the lush green valley below with its stands of the only recently discovered Wollemi pines, living fossils dating back to the age of the dinosaurs.

They arrived at their destination in well under ninety minutes, all the while keeping to the varying speed limits. The time had passed quickly as it always did when two like-minded people found themselves together. Growing up together, despite Brendon's seven-year seniority, the two of them had a great deal in common, not the least of it a passion for the Law. It was in their blood. Both had ambitions to become QCs. Brendon would take silk first. Brendon found he could talk to Charlotte as he couldn't talk to any of his girlfriends. The very attractive young women in his life were into fun, having a good time. Not that he was against that by any means, but any discussion coming around to criminal cases, however fascinating, wasn't high on the agenda. Charlie, on the other hand, liked nothing more than involving herself in such discussions.

The scrolled-iron gates were wide open. Charlotte as a courtesy had rung ahead.

"Well, we're here now," Brendon said, with a marked lack of enthusiasm. He didn't want to drive in. He thoroughly disliked Charlotte's uncle, and he was wary of Aunt Patricia with her flirtatious air, which he didn't find in the least bit appropriate or intriguing as she seemed to think.

The tall sandstone pillars on either side of the entrance were topped by handsome recumbent lions. They were supposed to be at rest, yet he always got the impression the lions were ready to spring, which was exactly what the late Sir Reginald would have wanted to think.

"What are *your* thoughts?" he asked as they cruised up the long, scenic drive. The Mansfield mountain retreat had been built on two secluded acres with wide expanses of lawn, beautiful trees, native and exotic and just about every flowering temperate shrub one could think of, azaleas, rhododendrons, camellias, and always a superb display of roses.

Charlotte darted him a faintly anxious look. "The same as yours, Bren. I've never felt welcome here since I lost my parents."

"Well, it's yours now," he said. "Aren't you tempted to kick your uncle out?"

"What, when he's working on another major novel?"

"Has anyone actually seen the working opus?" There was an acid edge to Brendon's voice.

"No one. I believe it's 'very closely guarded.' I think that's the right term."

"You realise it could all be untrue?" he said. "There *is* no follow-up bestseller."

Charlotte gave vent to a sigh. "I'd accept that without too much trouble. On the other hand, we could both be wrong. Major novels don't come overnight."

"His did. It wasn't all that long after the tragedy."

"Perhaps tragedy called it forth? I don't know. Perhaps writing a novel had always been his dream?" She shrugged. "I should start a book of my own. I can write, you know. I was too young at the time, but my father always had stacks of journals he kept in his study. What happened to them? They should have come to me. I would have treasured them."

"I've no idea what became of them, Charlie," Brendon said. He had gone looking for them as soon as he was able. "Everyone was in such shock at the time. Your father's papers, journals, and such like could have been cleared out. Someone could well have built a bonfire in the garden when Sir Reginald wasn't around. I do know all *relevant* documents were located and kept on file. They're all filed away at the office."

"I know. I've had a good look through them."

"Of course you have," he said dryly. "You're a sorter-outer."

"I have a need to know what's going on." Charlotte turned her head to study his clean-cut profile. "Aunt Patricia sounded delighted on the phone. Or she did when she realised I was bringing you. You're a great favourite with the ladies, Bren."

"Pretty easy where there's money," he said cynically.

"I dunno." Charlotte laughed. "Not in your case. You don't want to do this, do you?"

"You know I don't, Charlie. By the same token, you knew I wasn't going to let you to do it on your own."

Charlotte winced. "Your girlfriends must hate me," she said.

"What, you yell for help and I come?" he asked.

"Something like that. One of your girlfriends had the cheek to tell me I wasn't a sister who could expect devotion. I was no relation whatever. In short, I was taking up too much of your time."

He laughed. "I'm sure you jumped on her."

"I did respond rather sharply as it happens. I won't be inviting her to the party."

Brendon turned his head. "Who *was* that?"

"No one you'll miss terribly."

"Camilla?" he guessed correctly. Camilla had deeply resented his affection for Charlie.

"I've said all I'm saying." Then after a moment, "Had you no idea how jealous she was?" she asked with droll disdain.

"Most women are jealous creatures, aren't they?"

"Women don't go around killing their partners," she shot back.

Charlie took violence against women very seriously. "I know, Charlie," he said, gravely. A few months back, she had been asked her views on domestic violence by an enterprising reporter. As expected, she had given male violence a fine hammering.

The architect-designed sandstone house sat at the end of the long, gravelled drive. Clouds was a gabled, two-story residence that had all the charm one expects of a country house. A series of French glass doors opened onto a deeply shaded porch that allowed easy access to the lovely landscaped grounds. The breathtaking views of the mountains and the valley could be seen from every room at the *rear* of the house. Clouds was a splendid country residence that had only known one owner, Sir Reginald Mansfield. On his death he had bequeathed it to his granddaughter and heiress, the soon-to-turn-twenty-one Charlotte Mansfield.

The multiple garages were off to the left. They were joined to the house by a glorious wisteria-wreathed walkway. Brendon chose to park close to the short flight of front steps. "Let me get that," he said as Charlotte was having a struggle with her single piece of luggage.

"Okay, it's a bit heavy."

"A *bit?*" he growled as he pulled the suitcase out of the boot.

"I thought we'd have dinner in the village," Charlotte said. Bren was wonderful company. "You know. Touch glasses. Drink deep. Turn a few heads." Charlotte had become used to turning heads and hearing lots of gossip. It went with the territory.

"Fine by me." Brendon broke off as Patricia Mansfield, a vision in a multicoloured caftan, silver baubles swinging around her neck, emerged from the cool of the house. She tripped lightly down the steps, her attractive, cared-for face lit with welcome.

"Charlotte. Brendon. How lovely to see you!" she cried, like a woman enraptured by their arrival.

"Don't answer that," Charlotte whispered.

Patricia was upon them, reaching out to hug Charlotte—a first—before presenting her cheek, presumably for Brendon to kiss.

It was all so bizarre! Brendon wanted to step back, but that would have been too churlish. He bent his head, lightly grazing Patricia Mansfield's smooth, perfumed cheek.

Turning back to face Charlotte, Patricia enthused, "I've got a lovely surprise waiting for you, my dear. Simon is home."

Of all the dumb luck! "Simon is home?" Charlotte couldn't pretend she was thrilled. "And here I was thinking I had an extra sense," she said. "You can't have forgotten the last time I saw Simon, he was acting like he wanted to punch my face in. Now I'm supposed to be happy he's here?"

Simon's mother, as self-complacent a woman as one could find, pulled a little face. "Charlotte, dear, do let bygones be bygones. I'm willing. You do realize, I'm sure, that it was a devastating blow to us all. One has to make allowances. Simon adores his father. If he unfortunately showed too much anger that day, it was because he felt so deeply for his father."

"Are you telling us, Mrs. Mansfield, he's now over it?" Brendon asked, his tolerance for Patricia Mansfield wearing too thin, too soon.

Some expression flitted across Patricia Mansfield's face that was not easy to define. Was it disappointment? Wasn't Brendon's manner what she expected? "Goodness me, Brendon," she said. "I should think you'd be able to call me Patricia by now."

"*Why* exactly is Simon here?" Charlotte cut in bluntly. Was her aunt serious? Bren had to call her "Patricia" all of a sudden? She fought a flash of anger. Aunt Patricia should have told her about Simon on the phone.

Patricia gave a lighthearted laugh. Charlotte's disapproval was running off her like water off a duck's back. "Now, what do you think? Your twenty-first birthday, of course, dear girl. You will be having a big party, one assumes?"

"Why don't we go inside?" Brendon said, catching the fiery light in Charlotte's green eyes.

"Of course. Of course." Patricia, her complacence unruffled, turned to lead the way. "I've arranged for morning tea. You'll want to settle in. Why don't we all meet up in the living room in, say, half an hour?"

Charlotte had a ready answer, but she bit her tongue instead. Clearly Aunt Patricia had gotten into the habit of thinking the country house was hers. She hadn't really minded her uncle and aunt staying on at Clouds, but now she was beginning to think it was a huge mistake. Aunt Patricia obviously thought possession was nine-tenths of the law.

"Which bedrooms have been opened up for us?" Charlotte asked as her aunt started to move off.

Patricia turned to give her a brilliant smile. "The most beautiful one for you naturally, dear."

"You've moved out, then?" Charlotte couldn't resist the dig.

Her aunt stared back at her, startled. "Well, Conrad and I have been using the master suite for years now, dear, if that's what you mean."

"Why not?" said Charlotte. "The view is unequalled."

"The Blue Room and the Green Room have been prepared," Patricia informed them as they moved into the spacious stair hall with its polished floor partially covered by a beautiful contemporary turquoise rug. The rug, new to Charlotte's eyes, complemented the palette used throughout the rest of the house. White, blues, varying shades of green, all inspired by the mountain setting.

"I'm sure you'll be very happy there." Patricia Mansfield produced an indulgent smile, confident she was hiding her antipathy and, it had to be admitted, her wariness of Charlotte well.

"I'll let you know if we aren't," Charlotte replied. "The Green Room is fine, but I like to be within shouting distance of Bren. We'll check the room next door. Easy enough to air it out and make up the bed."

Patricia was jolted. "My dear, I've put Simon into the room next door to you. He's brought a friend, a lovely girl."

Charlotte blew out a breath. "You *are* a surprising lady, Aunt Patricia. I certainly don't disapprove of Simon's having a lovely girlfriend, but I could do without them in the room beside mine."

Brendon felt the need to intervene. "We're not really concerned, are we, Charlie?" he asked in a reasonable voice, when in reality he was as angry as Charlotte at the cavalier treatment they were receiving.

Charlotte turned to him. "As my closest friend, Brendon, I'm going to see you're as comfortable as you can be. I don't like to mention it, Aunt Patricia, but I come with the house. Perhaps you've forgotten?"

Patricia struggled hard to answer benignly, but was overcome by a rush of resentment for Alyssa's child, though Alyssa had never had such firepower. "And God bless you, my dear," she said smoothly. "Dear Sir Reginald will never die while you're around."

"Be sure of it," Charlotte replied. She longed to tell Patricia to her face that her mother, Alyssa, had never liked her. Her mother had believed her sister-in-law was both a liar and a troublemaker. One reason why her mother had avoided her, even though Charlotte remembered clearly Aunt Patricia's shock and grief at her parents' deaths. She had been as devastated by the disaster as the rest of them.

Brendon was still quietly laughing as they left Aunt Patricia and climbed the stairs to the upstairs gallery. "No wonder you don't call your aunt a friend."

"It's a sad fact that my mother kept her distance from her," Charlotte said.

"A lot was going on in those days, Charlie," he reminded her.

"You're right, of course. The thing is, Bren, I remember my mother and father as being a loving couple. All right, so they weren't living on top of one another. My mother made frequent escapes, but I never saw or heard any terrible fights until nearing the end. I'd never heard my mother being bitchy to my father, nor did I hear him offering her any kind of insult. Not long before they were killed, I surprised them kissing passionately. Yet my mother was supposed to be having a white-hot affair with *your* father?"

"Which he has always denied," Brendon said, his expression tightening.

"It would have been no easy thing to be accused of," Charlotte said. "Who was it who blew the whistle on them?"

Brendon followed Charlotte down the west wing. "We have no idea who started the rumours. I fancy someone who well knew how to remain anonymous. My dad put a stop to it all. He didn't call anyone out. He endured. He did *not* want out of his marriage. That was very clear. He had always given every appearance of loving my mother."

"Yet he broke her heart? It's a question that needs to be answered, Bren. One that's been hanging over our heads."

"It would take a miracle, Charlie, to find out the truth," he replied soberly.

"In the meantime we've lived a life full of secrets, seductions, and endless lies," Charlotte said. "It's a wonder we're not mortal enemies."

"We will be in a good minute if I can't put this suitcase down," he said briskly.

"Okay. Okay." Charlotte picked up her step. "I don't want to get too angry at this stage, Bren. I've allowed Uncle Conrad to stay, but it could have been a mistake."

"I'd say so from the way *Patricia* talks. Why didn't she give you the bad news over the phone?"

"That Simon is home?"

"Wherever 'home' might be. These past years your uncle has been acting like he's dependent on your grace and favour. It's ridiculous. He's sitting on twenty-five million."

"I know. But it was hard for him, with Poppa's sweeping him aside," Charlotte said, trying to be fair. "One would have thought he had my father killed the way Poppa reacted. We all know Poppa made doubly sure the wrecked Mercedes was thoroughly checked. Nothing suspicious was found. Poppa's attitude could be seen as terribly unfair to Uncle Conrad."

"No need for *you* to make amends," Brendon said. "The good news is, your uncle received enough of your grandfather's fortune to keep him in clover for the rest of his life. Now, where are these bedrooms? I haven't been here for years and years."

Charlotte gave him a quick smile. "I'm going to change all that. You can come here whenever you want to. You can bring some beautiful girl you really like. You can bring your super-bright male friends. In the springtime, when all the varieties of camellias, azaleas, and rhododendrons are out, I'm going to open the gardens back up to the public. Grandma Julia did that. I want to bring the custom back."

"Now, there was someone who really loved you," Brendon said.

"The loveliest woman you could ever meet," Charlotte said quietly, starting to slow as she passed the series of closed doors. "Why she ever married Poppa I'll never know."

Brendon nearly told her she wasn't on her own in that, but let it slide. Lady Julia Mansfield, the wife of Sir Reginald, never in robust health, had literally pined away after the violent death of her elder son. "Ironically, according to my grandfather, Sir Reginald as a young man was the answer to a maiden's prayer. Even as an old man he remained very upright, very handsome."

Charlotte appeared unimpressed. "Be that as it may, my grandmother would have been better off with just about any other admirer she knew."

An impressive truth. It was obvious from her remark that Charlotte still didn't know Sir Reginald had stolen away the love of his grandfather Hugo's life, right from under his nose. A huge betrayal of trust if ever there was one. The pain all these many years later was still there, although the subject was *never* mentioned. Indeed, he had never heard his grandfather utter Lady Julia's name.

*   *   *

The Green Room, so called because the colour scheme was a fresh lime green and white, had space enough for a chaise longue, a pretty little desk and chair, and a chest at the end of the bed. Two large matching framed photographs of the legendary Three Sisters hung on the wall behind the bed. All the bedrooms had their own en suite. The big picture windows that brought so much light into the large room afforded a superb panoramic view of the mountains and the valley. In the crystal-clear morning light, the blue haze lent an intriguing veil.

"I guess this will do," Charlotte said, turning back from the view to speak to Brendon. "Now, for you. I'm not happy about Aunt Patricia fixing up Simon and his girlfriend next door."

"It's not as though the walls are paper-thin," Brendon said dryly. "You're not going to toss them out, are you?" He searched her small, determined face. Although Charlotte had the Mansfield colouring, blond hair and green eyes, as she'd matured the looks of her beautiful mother, Alyssa, were coming through. It was all in the bone structure and the shallow cleft in her chin. One had to marvel at genetic encoding that reproduced physical features down the generations. Charlotte, like her mother, didn't have the Mansfield height. She was small-boned and petite. "Well?" He saw the brilliant look in her eyes.

"Once I would have jumped at the chance. I *would* do it if he hadn't brought his girlfriend." She shrugged. "He's a real—"

"*Charlotte!*" Charlie had a goodly selection of salty words learned at the shelters she visited on a regular basis.

"I nearly said it, but I didn't," she admitted. "Let's move on."

They walked down the corridor, Charlotte opening doors and peering in. Four doors down, she was satisfied. It was a spacious room like all the others, but the colour scheme held to off-white, with the large Outback painting on the wall lending vibrant colour. The ochres, the pinks, and the rusts were picked up by the cushions on the armchair and the pile on the bed. "This will suit me fine," Brendon said. "It's only one night anyway."

"So it's *not* fine?" She spun on him.

"Charlie, settle down. Everything is okay. Simon may have changed. Grown up."

"That would take a tectonic shift."

He felt so, too. "His girlfriend could be very nice."

Charlotte went quiet for a bit. "Wonderful luck for him if she is. Aunt Patricia seems to think they'll all be invited to my birthday party as a matter of course."

"You don't want them?" Inviting one's family was the usual thing.

"No. They were never there for me, Bren. You know that. The three of them put on a terrible song and dance when the will was read. You weren't there."

"Charlie, I *heard* all about it," he groaned. The anger and bitter resentment displayed by Charlotte's family had shocked a hitherto unshockable team of lawyers.

"Does a leopard ever change its spots? No, never," she said vehemently. "There are plenty of places around here to push me over a cliff and down into the valley. God knows the stakes are high enough."

In an instant all of Brendon's senses were on point. "Charlie!" For Charlie to be at peril! He went to her, pulled her to him, his chin resting on the top of her glimmering golden head. Her hair smelled wonderfully clean and fresh. "That's not going to happen," he said, with the rock-solid sense of commitment that defined him.

"I have dreams," she confessed. "They take me to the very edge of panic. In every one of them, I'm the prey."

"For God's sake!" He gathered her even closer. She was leaning into him so their bodies were touching. For a split second Brendon's heart gave a queer jerk. He was acutely aware of the feel of Charlotte—the exact shape of her—in his arms. He could feel a heat rising in him. Charlotte, for all her petite-ness, or perhaps because of it, seemed to *fit* him like no one else. He had to put a reason to it. He had known Charlie from childhood. Their bond had been forged over a very long time. Charlotte was "Charlie." All of a sudden, he felt compelled to remember it.

"It's a bit like having a price on your head," she was saying in a muffled voice.

He had never heard Charlotte sound so alone, so undefended. "No one is going to mess with you while I'm around, Charlie."

"You can't be on duty all the time."

"Yes, I can. Have faith in me."

"I do. I do." She wanted to stay there, safe, within Bren's strong arms, but she pulled back with a brief self-conscious laugh that wasn't usual. When had she ever felt self-conscious with Bren? "I can't explain my sudden vulnerability, even to myself. You'll get some practice protecting me, Bren. Mark my words."

He took a deep breath. "I *said* I'm ready for it. So you don't want your family, such as it is, at the party?"

"I do not." Her green eyes flashed.

"Of course they're expecting it to be held at a hotel. Two or three hundred guests."

"When I've wound the numbers down," she said.

"Do you intend asking my mother and father?" Brendon asked. "For that matter my grandfather, your guardian these past years?"

She met his silver-grey eyes. "I very much doubt you would come if I didn't."

"So, that's a yes?"

She turned to him, her body framed by the great sweeping, magnificent mountain views, lit by the light that streamed into the room. "Of course it's a yes. I'm not an ungrateful person. I suppose they have to be good people if you love them."

"I love you too, Charlie," he said, keeping to the same familial tone he always used with her.

A sad little smile played around her cushiony mouth. "The thing is, Bren, I don't think I know what love is."

Once her parents had gone, she had known precious little of it. "Coming here opens up old wounds," he said with concern.

"I feel it's necessary, Bren. Poppa thought it a good place to die. My parents died not all that far from here, down the mountain. I own this house free and clear. There are answers here. I intend to find them. The chinks in the armour that open up and as quickly close might become clear to me."

"Maybe you're frightened to remember what you believe you know? You were only twelve, Charlotte, but you weren't any ordinary twelve-year-old," Brendon said.

"It's called sublimation, isn't it? I know my mother didn't trust Aunt Patricia. I mean, she *really* didn't trust her. Why not? Things can never go back to the way they were when trust is lost. The relationship becomes different. What did Aunt Patricia do or say about my mother? She was always making little jokes that weren't in the least funny. I do remember Poppa once telling her very loudly to 'shut the hell up!' "

"I can imagine!" Bren exclaimed, visualizing the lion roaring. Sir Reginald cranky and displeased would have been something to see. "Jealousy, that might be the answer, Charlie. Your aunt didn't have your mother's beauty or charisma."

"And she could have had a hand in trying to destroy my mother's reputation," Charlotte said, with a kind of resigned sorrow. "If it's true, I will never accept it. We're close to what I want to know. They hate me. The affability is sheer window dressing. I can *never* trust them."

Her attitude was inherently dramatic, part and parcel of her passionate nature. "You don't trust my family, either, Charlie," Brendon reminded her. "But we're the ones who are going to keep you safe." It was a solemn vow.

Chapter 3

The family was assembled in the huge open-plan living room with the mountainous panorama a breathtaking backdrop. Conrad Mansfield; his wife, Patricia; their son, Simon, a good-looking young man with a thick thatch of gold hair streaked with flaxen, were in attendance. Simon was wearing his familiar supercilious expression. His girlfriend *was* a surprise. She was a complete departure from the glamorous, on-the-vapid-side socialites Simon had always favoured. She was seated in front of his standing figure in a pose reminiscent of a Victorian portrait with one of Simon's hands held firmly on her shoulder.

"My dear girl!" Uncle Conrad rose from his armchair, the genial host. Since Charlotte had last seen him, he had allowed his copious mane, a premature white, to grow long enough to form a ponytail. His beautifully trimmed darker beard and moustache only heightened the image of the literary lion, an image reinforced by his slightly eccentric but expensive clothing. Like his late father, Sir Reginald, the premature white was very flattering to his handsome, well-preserved face and his bright green eyes. He looked good. "How wonderful to see you, Charlotte," he enthused. A man determined to play it right. "You, too, Brendon."

It was an Academy Award performance, yet Charlotte felt as nervous as a high-strung cat. The earlier bout of panic was threatening to re-erupt. She couldn't allow that. It made her feel fragile. Her uncle might not have shown the slightest interest in her these past years, indeed her entire life, but he *was* her uncle, not a potential assassin. The thought calmed her. Her uncle hadn't been responsible for her parents' death. Her grandfather had simply made a ruthless decision in bypassing his remaining son as his heir. Obviously she had soaked up some of her grandfather's harsh attitude. Nevertheless, she wasn't going to play this monstrous game of happy families. It was sheer farce.

Brendon, at her side, had no difficulty reading Charlotte's body language. He stepped into the breach, taking Conrad Mansfield's outstretched hand. "It's a wonder you recognise me, sir," he said.

"You haven't changed since you were a boy," Conrad remarked in a resonant, cultured voice that filled Charlotte with poignant memories of her beloved father. The two brothers had shared a close physical resemblance. "I regret we haven't seen each other more often, Brendon. How's the family?"

"Always together," said Brendon suavely. He had no time for Charlotte's uncle, famous author or not.

Aunt Patricia broke in, winding her heavy necklace around her hand. "You haven't met Carol. Carol Sutton."

Both Charlotte and Brendon turned to smile in a friendly way at Simon's girlfriend. Carol Sutton looked charming. Certainly not one of Simon's glamour girls. She was well-dressed, if conservatively, for her age. Not a "looker," but *interesting*. She wore her dark hair in a standard pageboy. Her fine dark eyes were her best feature.

What was she doing with Simon? Charlotte very nearly shook her head.

"Gosh, ain't that grand!" Simon gave a sneer. "They actually like you, Caro, when I expected something quite different." He turned back to his mother. "You really should have left the introductions to me, Mother."

Patricia changed colour. "Whatever do you mean, darling?"

"I'm quite capable of introducing Carol, don't you think?"

"Good heavens, darling!" Patricia's smile shrivelled up.

"I'll tell you another thing," Simon continued on his merry way, his eyes locking on Charlotte.

Charlotte knew from long experience that Simon was preparing to go into one of his rants. He had been given to them as a child, when his bad behaviour went unaddressed. She put up a hand that nevertheless carried a clear message. "I can see where you're going, so I'll stop you there, Simon. That's if you ever wish to visit again. Do please sit down. I want to tell you all something."

"Of course you do!" Simon threw back his blond head. Any sort of reprimand, big or small, only encouraged him. "You are, after all, our little heiress."

"Indeed I am, and you're a guest in my house." Charlotte's tone was startlingly reminiscent of their late grandfather.

Everyone heard it, except Simon, who was both clever and thick. "Now, isn't she priceless!" he asked of no one in particular.

His father abruptly broke out of his role of genial host. "Sit down, Simon. Or leave." His eyes shifted to Carol Sutton, who seemed about to announce she had a splitting headache. "I'm so sorry, my dear. My son doesn't hide his feelings well."

"We were hoping, Simon, you'd come back reborn," Brendon said, a satirical twist to his mouth.

"I'll never be resigned to what happened to us!" Simon, who had a real gift for upsetting people, cried. "The unfairness of it all! It can never be forgotten or forgiven. How can we build a family on such foundations?"

"I agree it's hard when we're such a dysfunctional family," Charlotte said. "Only I can't feel sorry for you, Simon. Between ourselves you didn't go short."

"Peanuts compared to you!" Simon's dull flush reflected his anger. "Grandfather made a mistake. I was the senior grandchild. I mean, who are you? *What* are you?"

A dead silence greeted the absurdity of his questions. It was quickly broken by Brendon's searing comment. "Charlotte is your blood cousin. She is someone everyone admires. Your grandfather, as always, knew exactly what he was doing. Your father is a renowned author. He had no wish to remain in Chambers, did you, sir?"

"No, no," Conrad replied with the dignity of a born actor. "If we're talking frankly, I was never greatly interested in the Law."

"That's not the point, Dad!" Simon cried, bitterly disappointed in his father's perceived slackness. "Charlotte came between you and your rightful inheritance."

"I think I have no part in this discussion," Carol Sutton said very quietly. "If I may be excused?" She looked to Charlotte for a response.

"Please, Carol, stay," Charlotte urged, wondering if Aunt Patricia's idea of inviting her obnoxious son was a poor joke. "Simon has said all he's going to say."

"I want Carol here with me." Simon, who had no understanding of any point of view other than his own, increased the pressure on Carol's shoulder. To Charlotte's mind it was the action of a born controller. Just how well did Carol Sutton know her new boyfriend? She seemed a world away from his usual type.

"Let's all sit down, shall we?" she invited. "I need to talk to you about my twenty-first birthday party."

"I can't tell you how that has raised our spirits, dear." Patricia was off again in the guise of affectionate aunt. "I expect you'll hold it at . . ." She began to reel off the names of four gold-standard luxury hotels in Sydney.

"I don't want to do that at all, Aunt Patricia," Charlotte said, putting her aunt's speculations on the chopping block. "I don't want a big party. I'm having no more than forty or fifty guests. I intend to hold it here at Clouds."

The family, drawn together as one, looked severely taken aback.

"But I thought it was all settled," Patricia Mansfield cried, sounding bitterly disappointed in Charlotte's choice of venue. "There are so many people fond of you, Charlotte dear. We have so many friends in business and society. You have a name. You can't let people down. It wouldn't be fair of you, would it?"

Charlotte evaded the question. "Who told you it was all settled?" she asked.

Patricia looked at the ceiling as if waiting for a prompt.

"Surely Cynthia Bradford?" Conrad suggested sharply. "The Le Feuvres?"

"It really doesn't matter. They were only hoping or guessing," Charlotte said. "I'm as free as anyone else to decide on the venue. It will be here. That's why Brendon and I are here this weekend. We want to look over the house this very afternoon. Where they will all sleep can be worked out. I've already spoken to the proprietor of Blue Horizons."

Patricia's expression could only be described as *injured*. "Surely you could have spoken to me first, Charlotte?" According to her own lights, she had the perfect right to be consulted before any decision was made.

"I had already guessed your views, Aunt Patricia," Charlotte replied, wondering how best to tell them she didn't want them there.

She risked a glance at Brendon. His expression seemed to say, *You're stuck with them.*

Simon muttered something to his girlfriend, then moved back so precipitously he almost knocked the cover off a valuable spinach-jade incense burner on the circular table behind him. It was Carol who moved swiftly to right the tripod vessel.

"Do look what you're doing, Simon," his father said sharply. "That incense burner is quite valuable. It's Qing dynasty."

"Then it should be locked in a glass case," Simon retorted with a snort.

"As I recall, it *was*," Charlotte said. "I think it should go back into the case, along with the rest of Grandfather's collection."

"It's been perfectly safe up until now," Conrad Mansfield said with a flash of anger.

"That's right, apologize to her." Simon was determined to have his say. "I suppose she's going to tell us next she wants us to move out."

"It is possible, it could be *you*," Brendon pointed out.

Carol Sutton was looking more and more distressed. Clearly she had not known what she was in for. "I would do what you want to do, Charlotte," she said in a gentle voice. "It's your party."

She didn't earn a hug for that. Indeed, Simon gave her a quelling look. "Would you mind staying out of this, Caro?" he said, like a strict husband laying down the law.

"I'm sorry. I . . ." Carol's voice seemed to be lodged in her throat.

"What's the problem, Simon?" Brendon asked. "Carol is surely entitled to her opinion?"

"Carol doesn't understand the situation," said Simon.

"It must be made clear that a convivial atmosphere is essential for Charlotte's twenty-first," Brendon went on in his naturally authoritative way, which had been considerably strengthened by his professional life. "It's a once-in-a-lifetime celebration. You don't appear to accept that *you* are subject to custom and convention, Simon?"

"And who are *you*, exactly?" Simon burst out, unable to control the plethora of resentments that were crushing the life out of him. He had always been jealous of the brilliant Brendon Macmillan and all his accomplishments. "Charlotte's bloody minder?" he accused. "Got your eye on her, have you? I wouldn't put it past you."

Charlotte noted the silver flash in Brendon's eyes, the way his tall, super-fit body tensed. "No, Bren. You mustn't," she said quietly. "Can't answer the question?" Simon continued, passionately determined to have it out. He could *never* forget how his father had been denied the family fortune. How *he* had been denied it. Had things gone to plan, he would have been his father's heir, with all the power he craved coming to him as a matter of course. Instead Charlotte, a schoolgirl, had won the first prize. They had all missed the fact that dear, little motherless, fatherless Charlotte had been the old devil's favourite.

Conrad belatedly intervened. He pushed back in his heavy armchair. "You've excelled yourself, Simon, at creating disunity. Your mother and I were hoping for better. I suggest you go upstairs and pack."

"I'll help," Carol said quickly, her cheeks deeply flushed.

A strange expression came over Simon's face. "Who needs *you?*" He rounded on her with a startling look that held a degree of disgust. "You're a traitor."

Carol's expression passed from acute embarrassment to absolute distress. "Simon, *please.* You can't say that." In their relatively short relationship, she had never seen this side of Simon. She was shocked at the change in him. Nevertheless she put out a conciliatory hand.

Simon ignored it. "Find your own way back," he said.

"Are you serious?" Carol was wishing she had never come.

Simon's mother sat apparently deaf and dumb, her expression one of a woman trying not to fall off a crumbling cliff.

"The sooner you deal with yourself, Simon," his father clipped off, "the better."

"That's good coming from you, Dad," Simon retorted with high scorn. He looked back at his father as if he despised him. "All your talk of putting up a fight was nothing more than a blind."

"I think you're forgetting that your father *did* put up a fight," Brendon cut in. "He hired a battery of lawyers to contest the will."

"Sir Reginald knew what would happen," Conrad said. "He made sure the will was airtight."

"He did, sir," Brendon said. "Charlotte had been hoping the family had come to terms with that."

"*I* haven't!" Simon shouted. "I never will. I'll be out of here in under ten minutes."

"The clock's ticking," said Charlotte.

Simon swung back, his green eyes livid. "You're just like your scandalous mother."

Brendon didn't hesitate. He stood up like a man on the verge of walloping the offender.

Well aware of his anger, Carol loyally ranged herself beside Simon, taking his hand. "I'll be going with Simon, of course. I'll lend him a helping hand."

Conrad Mansfield actually nodded approval. Not so Simon's mother.

"How unpleasant is this?" Patricia asked explosively. "Simon has always taken family matters very seriously. I for one don't blame him for becoming so agitated."

"Well, you wouldn't, Aunt Patricia. I think you even condoned his childhood tantrums. I don't know why you invited him here this weekend," Charlotte said. "Simon will never change. He has an inflexible nature."

"Sometimes life is difficult, Charlotte." Patricia Mansfield's colour rose.

Carol, although she clung to Simon's hand, looked distressed and worried. "Thank you for inviting me, Mrs. Mansfield. It's as Simon said. There are so many family things I don't understand. Naturally I'll be returning to Sydney with him."

Charlotte spoke directly to the other young woman. "You're very welcome to stay, Carol, as my guest. You can drive back with us tomorrow."

Carol, whose complexion was returning to its normal hue, spoke as though she had come to a necessary decision. "Thank you so much, Charlotte. I do appreciate your offer, but my place is with Simon."

Her *place?* Charlotte recognized with dismay that Carol was highly vulnerable to control.

"So butt out, Charlotte," Simon said, suddenly mollified by his girlfriend's response. He knew she was in love with him.

"Right now you're the one who's butting out," Brendon said, taking a step towards him.

Patricia Mansfield abruptly roused herself. "This is not what I planned," she said, clearly upset at what was really, given her son's combative nature, a predictable turn of events.

"Do let's go, Simon," Carol urged in her gentle voice.

He fixed her with another of his quelling glances. "I *heard*," he gritted.

"Well, good-bye, everyone," Carol dared to say. "I'm so glad I met you all. So sorry it didn't turn out well."

Simon began to haul her away. "Oh, do give it a rest, Caro," he was saying to her in an oppressive voice. "No one is worth your attention."

"I hope you heard that, Patricia," Conrad said in a derisive tone after his son and girlfriend had left the room. Husband and wife met one another's eyes. "You didn't even teach our son rudimentary good manners."

Patricia was at least consistent in the championing of her son. "He doesn't know what he's saying," she replied. "You're so hard on him, Conrad."

That accusation nearly convulsed her husband. "*Hard* on him!" he exploded. "When my own father was nothing short of a dictator? I feel sorry for that poor girl, getting mixed up with Simon. He has the worst characteristics of both of us."

Never a truer word, thought Charlotte. "I could do with that cup of coffee that was on offer," she intervened, casting a glance at Brendon.

"I daresay Janet was too nervous to come in." Patricia was having difficulty keeping to a measured tone. "I'll go see to it now. First, though, I'll say good-bye to our son, our *only* child, might I remind you, Conrad."

"Well, whose decision was that?" he pounced. "Go to our only child, by all means," he said smoothly, "but first have Janet wheel in the coffee."

Patricia appeared shocked at her husband's disclosures. Indeed it was a fight to hold on to her dignity. "No good will come of this," she warned.

"I don't know how much Carol cares for Simon . . ." Charlotte ventured.

"They're about due to become engaged," Aunt Patricia snapped, thus settling the question.

"That's interesting," Charlotte said. "Simon has picked just the sort of young woman he requires for a *wife*." It all came back to control, and Simon was a controller. What sort of life would Carol have, married to such a man?

"You've never been fond of your cousin, have you, Charlotte?" Aunt Patricia said in bitter rebuke. "Isn't that perhaps the reason for your hostility?"

"What hostility?" Charlotte said. "I don't think that deserves a reply."

Patricia Mansfield's whole body stiffened. "It doesn't please me to tell you this, Charlotte, but your mother never made us welcome."

An arrow of light shot into Charlotte's mind. *Why do you see me as your enemy, Patricia? It's simply not true.* There were more chinks of light coming.

Conrad Mansfield sat forward in his armchair. "That's your aunt's version of it, my dear. Not mine. I never heard one unpleasant word from your mother. She was a most beautiful woman, destined like my poor brother to die young. You're starting to look a lot like her, do you know? The colouring has been masking it. Jealousy has terrible consequences."

A burning flush crept up Patricia's neck. It was obvious she wasn't having her best day. "What right have you to talk about jealousy?" she reproached her husband. "You had a pathological jealousy of Christopher."

"Which I will regret for the rest of my life," said Conrad Mansfield without hesitation. "The way our father treated us was conducive to that sort of thing. Chris was everything. I was nothing. But no excuses." He broke off at the sound of heavy footsteps on the hall staircase. "That will be our son leaving," he said dryly, "if you want to catch up with him, Patricia."

Patricia Mansfield fled the huge room as though her life had suddenly become just too hard.

At her departure, Charlotte rose to her feet, a tiny load lifted from her heart. At least her uncle had his deep regrets. "I'll go organize the coffee," she said with her natural resilience. "Aunt Patricia really should have known how Simon would react."

Charlotte and Brendon spent the afternoon walking around the house, which they both agreed was a wonderful place to hold a party. All the floors throughout the house were of polished honey-coloured timber.

They decided on a large area where the rugs could be rolled up and stored away for the evening to allow for dancing. The buffet had to be planned. Charlotte doubted Janet, who turned out to be a very nice, competent woman, could manage it on her own. She would need help from the village. Charlotte had already decided to give her carte blanche to order in the hams, turkeys, chickens, seafood, lobsters, crayfish, oysters, and all the ingredients that would be needed for the various accompanying dishes, hot and cold.

A well-stocked bar would be set up. No one would be *driving* home. She would leave the flowers to the two highly artistic ladies in the village who owned the most beautiful florist shop one could imagine. They knew what she liked. They would be very glad for such a big job. Charlotte liked to support the local community. Smartly uniformed waiters would be needed to pour the champagne. She would have no trouble finding them.

Both she and Bren had expected Aunt Patricia to tag along, but Patricia had stayed away, thus registering her upset and disapproval. Charlotte had long since decided Aunt Patricia was the sort of woman so self-satisfied she had no idea how much she was disliked. Uncle Conrad had locked himself away in his study, claiming he had work to do.

"I'd like to get into that study," Charlotte said. "It wasn't *War and Peace* he gave to the world. It was a highly successful novel his readership had reason to believe would be followed by a string of bestsellers."

"Ah yes, the book!" Brendon murmured. "I was hoping to trap him into telling us the basic premise of his new work, what stage he was at, but thought better of it."

"I don't think they're happy together," Charlotte mused.

"Happy! Of course they're not," Brendon said.

"So what's the problem? If they're unhappy, why don't they split up? A loveless marriage must be terrible for both parties. Maybe behind all the suavity Uncle Conrad is having a nervous breakdown? Or he's had one now that he finds inspiration has dried up."

"In which case he could pour all that unhappiness into a novel?" Brendon suggested. "The first book was brilliant, deeply moving, a bittersweet love story. Hard to believe he has such a lyrical inner voice. He had to have been very much in love with his heroine, Laura?"

"Who bears no resemblance whatever to his wife," Charlotte said.

Looking down at her, Brendon thought falling in love with Charlotte might well be a life-changing experience. She had changed into a very pretty short dress that showed off her lovely limbs to perfection. "You said it yourself, Patricia stays with him because of the money."

"Better to have peace of mind and freedom, surely? I'm going to take a very long time to get married. If ever. I don't trust men."

"There are a few good guys around," Brendon pointed out, dryly. "You have to experience *life*, Charlie. I know you love kids."

"There's a price on getting married and having children," Charlotte said, her views coloured by her contact with abused women and children terrified of their menfolk.

"There's a price on everything," Brendon reminded her gently, aware of her low opinion of men. Deep down Charlotte was the little girl who had lost both her parents in tragic circumstances. It was unbelievable the way her family had let her down. His mother had long called the Mansfields a "nest of vipers." He had always thought it a bit harsh. Sir Reginald had loved Charlotte as much as it was possible to love anyone above his son Christopher. It was true that Conrad in many ways had had a raw deal, but he hadn't been left penniless. As for plain bloody-minded Simon with his high and mighty manner, Brendon regretted, as did Charlotte, that Simon had drawn the gentle Carol Sutton into his web.

They were strolling through the beautiful shady part of the grounds, where the autumn-flowering sasanquas were still holding their exquisite blooms in all shades of pink and red. The lower branches had been trimmed to give the effect of small trees, which Brendon thought was very effective.

The spring flowering of the countless bushes of camellia japonica was sadly over, like the azaleas, the rhododendrons, and the wonderful peonies he remembered, but the great banks of hydrangea—some blue, some pink, some mauve with sections of greenish-white—were putting on a marvellous display. He had always liked their mopheads. The intoxicating scent of the massed gardenia shrubs wafted along with them. He reached out to pick a perfect white, waxy blossom that starred the glossy green foliage, passing it to Charlie. She bent her golden head to sniff its perfume, and then pushed the blossom into her hair.

"Perfect!" he said. "No wonder Paradise is traditionally described as a garden," he remarked, possessed by a strange sort of restlessness, even when he was at peace. Clouds' gardens had been started in the early days of her marriage by Lady Julia. They were her lasting legacy.

"There's always been a language of flowers," Charlotte said, as entranced by all the beauty around them as Brendon was. "Ancient Greece and Rome had their language, right through the Middle Ages to the so-called age of chivalry. The Victorians made a big deal of flower language. Passionate communications without a word being spoken. You should try it some time, Bren."

He gave her an indulgent smile. "That's a reach, though I have been known to send my female friends flowers."

"Lovely Lisa?" Charlotte teased.

"As a matter of fact, yes."

"As I said, I like Lisa. I'm inviting her to the party, okay?"

"If you must."

"Don't worry. I'm going to let you see the list."

"That *is* noble of you," he said dryly.

"Anyone else? Anyone you particularly care for I don't know about?"

He looked down at her with mocking eyes. "There is another woman. Not the one you think."

She came to a complete standstill. "Who? This is *serious*, Bren." She put great emphasis on the word *serious*.

"Our mystery woman." His silver-grey eyes glinted back at her.

"Do you love her?" Charlotte asked. "I'm not going to move until you tell me."

Now *he* got to smile. "I'm joking, Charlie. Love is madness."

Apparently satisfied with his answer, she sauntered on her way. "I agree. At least I think I do. All my girlfriends have steady boyfriends."

There was no trace of calculated coquetry in her voice. Charlie said it like it was. "You're surely not going to tell me you couldn't have any guy you want?"

"I'd have to be swept away, Bren," she confided with a certain measure of wonder at her own exacting and fastidious nature. "It hasn't happened yet, that's for sure. Maybe I'm a cold person? Alright, not cold, maybe cool at the core. Maybe it's because I wouldn't care for a man trying to rule me, let alone my ruling him. That's not on. Have you ever experienced the great tugs of the heart, Bren?"

It was a serious question. He had to pretend to consider. "A twinge or two. I've been happily attracted. Will that do?"

Charlotte let out a sigh. "It wouldn't do me."

"No need to tell me, Charlie," he said, very dryly. "It would be all or nothing for you."

"*And* you," she shot back. "We're alike."

They were coming into the full sunlight and the long, flowering rose gardens that spread their heady perfume over the entire estate. The rose gardens were flanked by beds glowing with a host of other lovely sensuous, summer-flowering plants.

"Grandma chose many of the old-fashioned roses you see for their beautiful perfume," Charlotte told him, as they walked slowly down the aisles. "Rosa Damascina grows on Omar Khayyam's grave, did you know?"

"I did *not* know that, Charlie," he said. "Roses do it for me." He stooped to savour the fragrance of the apricot Just Joey.

"They're your favourite flower?" Charlotte asked.

"Of course. They're glorious."

She smiled on him. "Who doesn't love a rose, especially the David Austin roses?"

"And your favourite?" He realized he wanted to know all there was to know about Charlotte. For some reason he thought she might name the exquisite camellia.

She surprised him as usual. "I love all flowers, Bren. I couldn't live without them. My grandmother created and tended this wonderful garden all her married life. It's a garden to dream in. Monet said his garden was his masterpiece. 'I must have flowers. Always and always flowers,' he said, but if you really want to know my favourite flower, it's the arum lily."

"Really? You mean, all those white lilies growing around the pond?"

Charlotte nodded. "I love white flowers in particular. The arum lily with its pure white, hood-shaped flowers has an architectural appeal for me. It was Yves Saint Laurent's favourite flower. I've loved them since I was a child. Grandma loved them, too, but like you, the roses were her favourites. There's a pink rose named after her. Lady Julia. That's it." She pointed to a beautiful tea rose of a delicate true pink. "Why don't we go and sit in the summer house?" she suggested.

"Why not? I don't fancy going back inside," Brendon answered in a brooding voice. "Your relatives are a weird lot."

"Yours are pretty mucked up, as well," she returned, tartly.

"Thank God for you and me," he said sardonically, taking her arm. "So what's the betting Simon is made to apologize so he can get invited to the party? Whatever he *says*, he couldn't bear to be left out. He's such a snob."

"What's he got to be snobbish about? I hate pretentious people and I've met a few. I've the idea our Simon didn't make it in the Big Apple."

"He won't tell it that way," Brendon said in an educated guess.

The summer house was a romantic small structure at the bottom of the garden. It was the ideal place for quiet contemplation. Surrounded by mature shrubs, in this case the gorgeously scented, drooping white and purple wisteria, it offered repose. The bell-shaped roof and finial over the retreat had mellowed over time to a soft blue-grey. White fluted posts held up the structure, with five of its arched bays enclosed by white lattice that invited one in.

Together they walked into the cool, perfumed interior, Charlotte with her lovely light girlish movements, Brendon so much taller and stronger not far behind her. A slated white bench encircled the area with a box nearby that contained an array of plump cushions.

"I used to come here often," Charlotte remarked, waiting for Brendon to cover the hard slats with a few cushions. "I must have been the world's loneliest kid." To her consternation, her voice wavered a little, so she broke off. She prided herself on being made of sterner stuff.

"You always mattered to me, Charlie," Brendon said. Nothing else on earth mattered more to a child than a loving mother and father, he thought. Even *one* surviving parent. Charlotte had not been so lucky. Her cousin, Simon, had been doted on by his mother. He knew how much his own parents loved him, how proud they were of him. Charlie's happiest school vacations would have been spent with one or other of her school friends, all vetted carefully by her grandfather. It would have been so much different if his own mother had taken Charlie under her wing. Inexplicably she had not. Maybe she saw too much of the beautiful Alyssa in Charlie? God knows what the true story had been. He feared it would never be told.

"What are you thinking about?" Charlotte asked, reading his sombre expression.

"Looking back," he said.

"On the things I've missed?"

"Charlie," he said supportively, "there are going to be great things for you in the future."

She smiled an enigmatic little smile, taking a seat and settling her short skirt, which exposed her knees and slender legs. "Lovely old you! As long as I count, Bren. As long as I can do some good. I've got too much money. It's more a great burden than a reward. I know how Sir Hugo has everyone who comes in contact with me checked out."

"For your own safety," Bren said quietly, joining her on the bench. For years past his grandfather had had a series of "minders" in place. They were so good at going unnoticed, Charlotte would have had no idea she was being watched over.

"It's not safe to be an heiress," she said, thinking of past tragedies she had read about.

"You're a lot safer than some innocent young woman snatched off the street," he pointed out. "You're a lot safer in this country than anywhere else."

"There's that." She nodded her agreement. "Don't mind me, Bren. With an approaching milestone birthday, I'm feeling a bit emotional."

"Why wouldn't you be?" he said, his illusions about families staying together, long destroyed.

"Yes." She took the camellia he had given her out of her hair and began twirling it around in her fingers. "I sometimes think I might not ever get what I want."

"Do you know what you want, Charlie?" he asked.

"Life. Ordinary, love-filled life. Love is the flower of life. It's a vision. It's a . . ." She broke off, as involuntary tears sprang into her beautiful emerald-green eyes.

"Charlie!" His heart smote him. He had never seen Charlie cry. Not at the funerals of her parents. Not at the very public funeral of Sir Reginald. Those tears had been dammed up, but surely the dam had to be full to bursting point? On impulse he leaned sideways, intending to kiss her smooth cheek, only simultaneously she turned her blond head.

What happened next came as a shock to both of them. The chaste kiss Brendon had intended landed directly on her full-lipped, parted mouth. The thrill of impact was *enormous*. It strained every bit of Brendon's willpower not to deepen this kiss that was already perilously on the brink of becoming intense. Her lips seemed to part even more. That excited and moved him unbearably. This wasn't the gentle understanding kiss of a long, close friendship. This wasn't a "cousinly" kiss. His heart was beating violently. He had the wildest impulse to pull her across his knees, make love to her—to *her*, little Charlie—in the dazzling afternoon light. It was proving extraordinarily difficult to let her go.

Both tripped each other up to speak. "There's nothing like a kiss, is there?" Charlotte quavered, visibly unnerved.

"Well, you would turn your head," he said, shaken right out of his normal composure. "I don't think you need ever worry about being a *cold* person."

"I'm never cold with you, Bren," Charlotte said. "You were my one ray of sunshine for yonks. As a matter of fact"—she was getting her breath back—"as an unintended little peck, it was pretty good." Trying hard not to show her wildly unruly emotions, Charlotte sat upright, locking her hands together. "You might not guess this, but that was my very first kiss. A good thing I'll be able to remember it with pleasure."

"Your *first* kiss?" It wasn't like Charlie to tell a lie. "Charlie, I can*not* believe you've never been kissed." In his view she was a natural. He had never received such pleasure from a single kiss.

"Believe what you like," she said, tilting back her golden head. "I'm a very old-fashioned girl. Besides, I have a need to always be safe. My generation of friends wants everything at once. A lot of the girls I know believe they have to accede to whatever their boyfriends want, and we all know what that is. I'm *different*, Bren. There's plenty of time for me to get into sex if I want it. First I have to be sure. That kiss was *real*, wasn't it, Bren?"

He should have said, "*You know it was.*" Instead he backed off. "Kisses can be dangerous, Charlotte."

A faint shiver ran through her. "You mean, we're living with the memory of the sins of our family? Dangerous kisses lead to dangerous sex?" she asked. "The dangerous things that were done in the past?"

"We have to forget that, Charlotte," he warned. "We've passed the test of friendship. Of bonding. We look out for one another."

"Well, you look out for me," Charlotte said and stood up. "Why don't we go back to the house? Is dinner in the village still on?"

A deep seriousness had fallen on him. "Are you going to make me pay for kissing you, even if it was mostly your fault?" he asked.

She only smiled enigmatically. "I'm not going to allow anything to mess with what we have, Bren. I can't lose my dearest friend."

"Then dinner is still on," he said.

"And an end to kissing." She could say that, when she could still feel the warmth of Bren's sculpted mouth on her own. The sensations that had shot through her lingered, the near-painful leap of her heart, the sharp little prickles that ran through her body, deepening the further down they went. There wasn't going to be a simple solution. In a few unplanned moments they had crossed over a line from which there might be no coming back.

Chapter 4

The jacarandas had been slow to bloom that year. By mid-November, though, the entire city was awash with the city's purple "Christmas" trees. They were out in all their glory in the suburbs, the front yards, backyards, parks, streets, schools. A magnificent specimen flourished at the city's famous Circular Quay, the hub of Sydney Harbour, with wonderful views of the Harbour Bridge and a lovely walkway to the Opera House.

As happened in Queensland, the blossoming of the jacarandas signalled the posting of high school and University results. Charlotte received a huge buzz when she was awarded her bachelor of laws with honours. As a further bonus for all her hard work, she had emerged top of her class, something that had put at least two of her male colleagues' noses out of joint. Word of her high standing had gone out to the top law firms around the country. It was thought by no means certain that Charlotte Mansfield, granddaughter of the late Sir Reginald Mansfield, would enter the law chambers he had founded with Sir Hugo Macmillan, both men having been knighted for their services to the law not long before the honours system had been scrapped by the then labour prime minister. There were those who knew there had been many tensions between the two families. Plenty of gossip, rumour, speculation. Further, Sir Hugo's grandson, Brendon Macmillan, was making a name for himself as a formidable young barrister and future candidate for Queen's Counsel. There could be further clashes in store for the Mansfields and the Macmillans as Ms. Mansfield was well known to be equally as ambitious.

The end-of-year celebrations had started. Parties were held. Charlotte attended quite a few of them with a bodyguard, still unbeknownst to her, close by. Everything was in place for her twenty-first. Her dress had been delivered, a real sparkler, iridescent green covered by multicoloured sequins and beads. With it she planned to wear her grandmother Julia's multicoloured necklace of precious and semi-precious stones. The pièce de résistance would be appended to it, an enhancer featuring a large diamond daisy. The daisy would fall neatly into the vee of her cleavage. More than ever before, she wanted to look glamorous on her night of nights. She knew her girl-friends, all of whom Brendon knew, would be going all out to draw attention. Well, they had better move over. She was the belle of the ball. Nothing was going to spoil her big night.

A magnificent Christmas tree stood in the entrance hall of Clouds, decorated with all manner of glittering baubles. An exquisite little antique white porcelain angel with golden wings, holding her golden harp, topped the tree less than a foot below the high ceiling. It was Brendon who had offered to help Charlotte decorate the tree she had ordered: the quintessential Christmas tree, a European silver fir.

Artificial as it had to be, it captured perfectly in colour and texture the real thing. Charlotte left Brendon temporarily to it while she had a word with Aunt Patricia in the living room.

Aunt Patricia had not been pleased at Charlotte and Brendon's turning up on that Saturday, though she had done her best to hide it. It seemed from henceforth their every meeting would be a challenge, Charlotte thought.

"That tree is much too big, Charlotte," Patricia Mansfield gave her unsolicited opinion as though astonished at Charlotte's choice. She waved Charlotte into an armchair. "Worse, it will drop its needles all over the floor of the entrance hall, making such a mess! Especially for the party."

Charlotte tried her best to answer politely. This was the season of goodwill, after all. "It's *artificial*, Aunt Patricia, though I can see why you thought it wasn't. It captures perfectly the colour and texture of the real thing. I don't like to speak bluntly, but you leave me little option except to point out that this house is mine. As a courtesy, I have let you know when I'm coming, but I don't expect to be treated like an unwelcome guest when I arrive."

Patricia Mansfield wasn't accustomed to having salvos fired at her. "My dear girl, that's simply not true," she exclaimed, adopting a wounded expression. "I wonder how you can suggest it. Surely as your uncle and I live here, I'm entitled to my concerns. I really did think the tree was *real*."

"Then I got my money's worth," Charlotte said. "I know you and Uncle Conrad love living here at Clouds. Who would blame you? But it's not the only house in the world, Aunt Patricia. There are beautiful houses and apartments overlooking the harbour. So they carry a big price tag! Uncle Conrad is well able to afford a mansion." Even two. One for each of them.

Patricia Mansfield's arched brows shot even higher. "You may well point that out," she said, wondering which way was best to handle this imperious young woman who was looking more and more like her late, too-often-remembered mother. "But where else would your uncle get the peace and quiet to write his book?"

"You've read some of the unfinished manuscript?" Charlotte seized the opportunity to ask.

Patricia flushed and pinched in her lips. "Of course I have."

"Lucky you! What's the working title? *Cries of the Heart* was a great title."

Patricia Mansfield gave Charlotte a withering look. "Your uncle has a splendid mind."

"My *father* had a splendid mind, too," Charlotte said, aware that little chinks of light were opening up in her head again. "How I wish he and my mother were here with me today," she breathed. "You didn't like my mother, did you, Aunt Patricia?"

Patricia Mansfield stared across at Charlotte, her expression frozen. "How could you accuse me of that, Charlotte?" she said, clearing her throat with a slight choke. "I was devastated by Alyssa's death. I suppose your mother never told you it was she who disliked me, when I so wished everything could have been different. She didn't want your uncle or me getting too fond of you, either."

"When I thought you did it on purpose!" Charlotte said. "The thing is, I don't believe you, Aunt Patricia. For some reason I've been experiencing a lot of flashbacks these days. Or perhaps they've been there all along, but I chose to be blind. I can *hear* my mother speaking. I swear I remember my father using the exact words '*cries of the heart*,' which Uncle Conrad obviously picked up and used. My father was passionately in love with my mother."

"Which made her adultery all the more painful," Patricia shot back with barely disguised satisfaction. "We all wanted to spare you the fact your mother and your self-appointed protector, Brendon Macmillan's father, were having an affair."

"Malicious *rumour* said they were having an affair. I *don't* accept it. Neither does Bren."

Patricia gave a tight smile. "I understand that. Your loyalty is to be expected. I hope you realize, Charlotte, that the young man has his aspirations?"

"Of course he does. Eventually he hopes to take silk. No one doubts he will."

"His family would be pushing him to get closer to you, Charlotte," Patricia Mansfield said, apparently warning Charlotte of her fears. "You're supposed to be highly intelligent. You can see where I'm going?"

"Do please put it more plainly," Charlotte invited, outwardly calm, inwardly getting angrier by the minute. "I don't care for innuendo."

"My dear Charlotte, what I'm saying can't be unexpected. The Macmillans will be looking for a union of the two families. Many women, I believe, have succumbed to Brendon Macmillan's undoubted charms—"

"*You* being one of them, Aunt Patricia?"

"I hope I comport myself with elegant manners," Patricia said, completely unfazed. "Too few do these days. My impeccable behaviour is unsurpassed. I'm always pleasant to Brendon, my dear."

"But you're warning me against him, is that right?" Charlotte asked, caustically.

"In the absence of your mother, I regard it as a duty," Patricia declared. "The Macmillans are highly enough placed, but if Brendon were to marry you it would raise the level, don't you agree? In no time at all, the Macmillans would be controlling the Mansfield fortune."

Charlotte felt a white-hot jolt of anger, but she held on to it, mainly because Brendon was in the house. "I can't feel you have any right whatever to interfere in my life, Aunt Patricia. You made yourself too scarce. You can *never* speak or act for my mother. I *know* you disliked her. Maybe even hated her?"

Anger sharpened Patricia's features. "This when I'm only trying to help you, Charlotte?" she said, in her unassailable, arrogant way. "I held your mother in the highest regard until we as a family found out about the affair. It was never spoken about, but Alyssa could have been planning to leave Christopher and take you with her. She must have known all along she was skirting disaster. Then it happened. Your uncle and I have always believed your parents got into an argument in the car. One could have struck out at the other for all we know. The rest is history and our family's tragedy."

"You may have convinced yourself of this, but you haven't convinced me," Charlotte was quick to reply. "Poppa wasn't convinced, either. You'll remember, he had the Mercedes taken apart."

"Only to find absolutely nothing mechanically wrong. It was a dreadful accident. Your grandfather took it out on your innocent uncle for being the one to survive. Conrad had to bear the brunt. We all knew Christopher was the 'chosen one.' "

On impulse, Charlotte went a step further. "Did you hate my father, too?"

Patricia burst into shocked laughter. "I'll forget you said that, Charlotte. You're quite wrong and you show no respect. You have no realisation of how your uncle and I were made to feel. Not even second best. Your cousin, Simon, the perfect boy, overlooked for you!"

"It's what our grandfather wanted," Charlotte said. "Your 'perfect boy' has an offensive manner, Aunt."

"Oh, Charlotte, Charlotte!" There was a bitterly disappointed break in Patricia Mansfield's voice. "I know for a fact that people find Simon utterly charming."

"Was that in New York, was it?" Charlotte asked. "It certainly isn't here. Simon had better come down from his very high horse if he wants to be liked. He did ring to ask if he and Carol are invited to the party."

"And?"

The question had a placid, accepting sound. "I said *no.* I don't want my party to turn into a fight zone. Sadly, Simon is not capable of your unsurpassed, impeccable behaviour, Aunt Patricia."

"You mean, you won't let him in?" Patricia Mansfield flushed darkly.

"Call it a desire to have my twenty-first go well. A few drinks in, and Simon will be telling everyone how he was robbed. And it's *he,* you know. Simon isn't unhappy about what happened to his father. It's what happened to *him.* It's time you took the blindfold off regarding Simon, Aunt Patricia. You and Uncle Conrad are invited, as you know. If you're unhappy about Simon's exclusion and you find yourselves unable to attend, I accept that. Now, I must get back to Brendon. I'm supposed to be helping him decorate the tree."

Patricia Mansfield considered Charlotte with a look of great irony. "That's not his only mission, my dear," she said.

Brendon was whistling softly to himself as he went about decorating the tree. "You took your time," he said, as Charlotte joined him. "Everything okay?" He searched her face.

"Everything's great."

He knew at once it wasn't. "You told her about Simon?"

"You mean, the *perfect boy,* now the *perfect young man*?"

"And what did your aunt have to answer?"

"As expected, she was upset. Am I being selfish, Bren?" She had a great desire to become a woman of integrity. She wanted her dead parents, Poppa, and Grandma Julia to be proud of her.

"God, no!" Brendon reacted forcefully. "Simon can't keep his unfortunate mouth shut for five minutes. He was robbed of a fortune, you know."

"That's the way they see it."

"Move them out," Brendon advised. "Maybe not tomorrow, but early in the New Year. Get a married couple to come in as caretakers. There must be a couple you could trust in the village who'd jump at the chance."

"I know that. The Devlins would be perfect. That's if they're prepared to take on the job. Paddy knows all there is to know about roses. He worked here, you know. I remember all the great conversations he and Grandma used to have. He left when Grandma died. It's a big decision turning my own uncle out, rich man or not. By the way, Aunt Patricia claims to have read chapters of the new book," she confided in a low voice.

"Why should we believe her?" Brendon asked cynically, hooking on another frosted silver bauble. "Well?" He looked down at her in her summery white cotton and lace dress.

"Actually, I *don't*. I'm going to tell you another very strange thing."

"You're kidding me," Brendon mocked, though he was paying close attention.

"I seem to remember my father saying certain words to me. We were alone together. My mother had fled into Sydney. He said, '*Cries of the heart, Charlie, my darling. Cries of the heart.*'" As she spoke, her voice sank to a near whisper.

"Good God!" Brendon stared down at her, clearly startled.

"At least I *think* I remember it. These moments come, and then they slip away again. I had to have been a traumatized child. I can't tell you why, but something about Uncle Conrad frightens me." She looked up into his dynamic face. "You don't seem surprised, Bren." All of a sudden, her heart was beating suffocatingly.

Brendon saw it in the way her face suddenly paled. At once he put his arm around her. "Charlie, baby, what's the matter?"

His tone was so kind, so supportive, so *natural*, her sudden turmoil began to subside. A stolen kiss would have been divine at that point. It was what she had come to realize she craved, but she didn't suppose Brendon wanted to allow the *feeling* that had sprung up between them to burst into something uncontrollable, further ripping their families apart. Even the way he called her "baby" put out the flame. He had started calling her "*Charlie, baby*" when she was about six.

"One of your little chinks opening up?" he asked quietly.

She raised her head. "If I only knew the truth! It must be the same for you, Bren. Both of our parents maligned, most likely wrongfully. Unscrupulous people can do terrible things. They can cause untold misery. Telling terrible lies in an effort to destroy reputations is little short of criminal."

"Well, you know what they say, Charlie," he answered. "The truth will out. It may take a long time, but it will happen. Now, stop making yourself miserable." He gave her a brief hug that had a lot of affection in it. "We have a tree to finish."

Patricia Mansfield chose, or was *waiting* for, that exact moment to enter the stair hall. "I thought decorating the tree was the plan?" She gave a little tinkling laugh that could never be mistaken for pleasant. It was as insinuating as it could be.

Brendon took on a highly formidable stance. "Trust me, Patricia," he said in a tone that said, *Stay clear.* "I won't ever stand by and see Charlie hurt."

Patricia dared a mild sneer. "Your little ewe lamb, is she?"

"Please don't insult me or Charlotte."

Patricia Mansfield moved to the base of the staircase. "Brendon, dear, can't you take a joke? I wouldn't dream of insulting you. You mistake me." She glanced over at the half-decorated tree, looking genuinely delighted. "I'm so glad you stuck to a silver and gold colour scheme. So elegant, all the little lights twinkling like stars. It's going to look *marvellous* when you're finished. As you have so much influence with Charlotte, I'd be enormously grateful, Brendon, if you could convince her that Simon should be admitted to the party. He's *family*." With that, she took her first step up the stairs.

Her uncle and aunt had shown their upset and disapproval at Simon's being barred from Charlotte's party by booking into a luxury Sydney hotel for the weekend. The Macmillans, Sir Hugo, Brendon's parents, Julian and Olivia, arrived in a chauffeur-driven Rolls-Royce belonging to Sir Hugo. They stayed for a surprisingly pleasant hour or so, and then the waiting chauffeur drove them back to Sydney.

"We know the party is all about young people," Sir Hugo said. "So it's good night." He took Charlotte by her slim shoulders, leaning down to kiss her on both cheeks. "You're a fine young woman, Charlotte. Your grandfather, Lady Julia, and your parents would be very proud of you."

It was the first time either Brendon, standing nearby, or Charlotte had ever heard Sir Hugo mention Lady Julia. "Thank you, Sir Hugo," Charlotte said. "Thank you for everything you've done for me."

Sir Hugo beamed down on her. "It's been an honour, my dear. You can always come to me at any time. My door will always be open."

Charlotte had to rest content with Olivia Macmillan's cool parting kiss, something Olivia had always fought shy of. Olivia had held to her familiar reserve, but she looked regal in a long, form-fitting deep blue gown. Brendon's father, Julian, a very handsome man who had handed down his finely hewn features to his son, was far more expansive. At the last moment, he made the startling comment that she reminded him very much "of your beautiful mother, Alyssa."

Why exactly did he say that? Inflammatory stuff, surely? Especially in front of his ice-cold wife. Brendon escorted his family to Sir Hugo's parked Rolls-Royce while Charlotte stood perfectly still for a moment, trying to understand why Julian Mansfield had chosen to speak of *Alyssa*. For that matter, that night was also the first time Sir Hugo had spoken her grandmother's name. *Julia.* Did the menfolk, if not Brendon's mother, have a vision of her and Brendon together? Was Aunt Patricia right? Was she too quietly trusting? Imagine Brendon, the man she trusted most in the world, being part of that agenda? Having thought that even momentarily, she was seized by a sudden attack of shame for her disloyalty. Honour was honour, and Bren was an honourable man.

By ten o'clock the party was underway. Charlotte saw with pleasure that her guests were having a wonderful time. The hired three-piece band was excellent—it had to be at the price—having no trouble handling the numerous requests. Those who took to the dance floor were enjoying themselves both sweetly and immensely. No young man feeling the effects of the best French champagne had to be curbed as he would have been if trouble was in the air. This was a night that had to be remembered as fabulous and so much fun.

Charlotte had no difficulty picking out Brendon's crow-black head, he was so tall. His thick hair, worn longer than most, was curling up at the edge of his pristine white dress shirt.

The young woman he was dancing with was Lovely Lisa. She certainly lived up to that nickname. Tonight she wore a short, strapless gown the exact shade of her beautiful sapphire earrings. They had been dancing around for ages. Charlotte should have been happier about that, but she wasn't.

The dress code for the men was black tie, evening dress for the women; consequently everyone was looking their sophisticated best. The couple beside Bren and Lisa twirled away so she could get a good look at Lovely Lisa's face.

Oh hell!

Lisa was gazing up at Brendon, her big blue eyes drowning in adoration. Lisa wasn't only lovely to look at, she was a genuine darling. Charlotte had to blink several times. The image they presented was that of the perfect couple. Lisa was tilting her shining dark head back, laughing at something Brendon had said. She looked alight with happiness, which made Charlotte feel vaguely upset. She took a deep breath. This would never do. It took a huge effort, but she spun on her Valentino stilettos, open-toed, gold satin, embellished with crystals. The heels gave her over three inches. They were worth every penny. She knew without being told—which, of course, she was—her short glitter dress was perfect for her. Grandma's jewellery, needless to say, got more than its fair share of full-on inspections.

It was proving very difficult to get to the birthday girl, Brendon thought in frustration, and he was watching her like a hawk. She no sooner finished dancing with one of her admirers than another caught her up. All the young women at the party looked incredibly attractive in their beautiful party dresses, but Charlotte outshone them all, he decided. There wasn't much of her glittering dress, but what there was suited her to perfection. Lady Julia's jewellery couldn't have found a better home, especially the diamond daisy that fell between Charlotte's small, perfect breasts. He was a bit worried by her evening sandals. Stunning though they were, they were very high. She could twist her ankle dancing. Not that she did. She was naturally graceful. Her green eyes were sparkling like emeralds, her lovely skin flushed over her high cheekbones. A radiance was streaming from her. It was important to him that Charlie have a wonderful twenty-first birthday party, one to remember. He was about to move to her side, not prepared to take no for an answer, when the front man of the group announced a tango.

How about that! He had never been one to stay clear of the dance floor. He was sure he could put on a good enough show. He knew Charlie would. There wasn't an awkward bone in her body. God knew she had attended ballet classes for years on end. He had even been dragooned into showing up for a few incredibly boring recitals until Charlie came on. Now she lifted her golden head to announce there would be a prize, which she would present, for the best performance. A bottle of Bollinger, James Bond's favourite.

The next few minutes saw a mad rush to select the best dancing partners. No one seemed to give a toss about possible wounded feelings. In the nick of time Brendon was at Charlotte's side, watching a trio of admirers retreat to find other partners ASAP.

"Sure you can do this?" She tilted her gleaming head back to tease him.

He looked down at her. "Charlie, this is my favourite dance."

"Since when?" She laughed.

"Do I detect mockery in your tone?" He put one arm around her.

"Since the tango was announced. I can't guarantee I can pull it off as well as Colin Firth in some movie I saw, but I'll give it a go."

"Shouldn't you have asked Lisa?" she whispered, as Lisa was making no secret of her disappointment.

He leaned down and put his mouth to her ear. "Let's just say you're the better dancer."

"Well, to business," Charlotte said. "We have to give off a passionate vibe, you know. It's obligatory. Plenty of sexual energy. I'm not flustered. Are you up for it?"

"Don't worry about me," he bid her briefly. "Worry about yourself."

"Right." Put on her mettle, Charlotte took a great lungful of air. She would need it.

The trio started with tremendous *brio* into arguably the best modern tango song there was: "*La Cumparsita.*" It had been a big international hit for Julio Iglesias.

Brendon put his arm around Charlotte's tiny waist, gripped her tight. Her whole body was abuzz. He could feel it like an electric charge. All around them couples were doing the same thing. This was their moment. They took it.

"Gosh, have you ever seen anything like that?" Lisa's partner, not big on sensitivity, muttered in her delicate shell of an ear. "Didn't you tell me they're *cousins*? Look more like lovers."

Lisa didn't answer. Her lips trembled into a smile. "We can't possibly match them," she said. Other couples around them were arriving at the same conclusion, because after a while they stopped dancing, two by two, falling back to form a semicircle around the most accomplished couple. That no other dancers had any chance at all was the general opinion.

Charlotte and Brendon had forgotten everything but the dance. Their bodies bent and dipped, their legs extended this way and that, and their faces turned closely into one another's with an agitated but controlled passion, their heads at just the right angle. They even came close to kissing at one point. It was fantastic. Charlotte played the temptress. Brendon, throbbing with passion, was the man to tame her. Real life was suspended. That was the role of the dance.

"Anyone would think they were a couple of professionals." Lisa's companion finally became aware Lisa wasn't really enjoying the mesmerizing performance. He knew Lisa had once been madly in love with Macmillan, the handsome devil. Dance routine or not—in his view, they were showing off—there was a tremendous amount of *sex* tied in to the physical adroitness. The birthday girl looked positively delectable, he thought, the perfect object of her partner's passion. Of course, the two of them were determined to win, he thought. That's who the Mansfields and the Macmillans were. Winners in their public and private lives.

The dance finished in spectacular fashion, with Brendon's strength only increasing, holding Charlotte in a challenging arched-back position with her golden head only inches from the polished floor. There were a few gasps, as though she might crash, but no such thing happened. Charlotte looked perfectly secure. There was an instant of crackling silence, and then happy, laughing faces, ringing cheers, and loud applause that rolled in waves around the room. A few of the young men gave in to the temptation to piercingly whistle their appreciation. The impressive, very sexy performance had certainly upped the already high-voltage mood of the party.

"Okay?" Brendon asked Charlotte as he brought her gracefully to her feet.

"Brilliant!" she said, when in truth she was breathless. "All those ballet lessons finally paid off."

The buffet table was groaning beneath the weight of sumptuous dishes, hot and cold. Waiters circled, filling and refilling crystal flutes with champagne. Some of the young men preferred ice-cold beers. Those beverages too were supplied, as well as frosty cold soft drinks and juices. Everyone, including the most diet-conscious guests, put their diets aside just this once.

Outside in the entrance hall, the great Christmas tree shimmered and glittered, the countless tiny LED lights twinkling like stars amid the green needles of the fir tree. Circling the tree were Charlotte's birthday presents, extravagantly wrapped in richly patterned papers and ribbons. Charlotte had invited the trio to the buffet. In the absence of their music-making, Christmas carols were being piped softly through the house.

The sweets table, covered in starched white linen, looked irresistible: cheesecakes decorated with kiwi fruit and all the red berries piped with whipped cream. There were baby pavlovas, trifles, variations of the always-popular tiramisu and crème brûlée tarts. There were even frozen ricotta cakes that disappeared before they could melt.

To cap it all was Charlotte's twenty-first birthday cake, a magnificent four-tiered chocolate-raspberry cake made by a lady in the village renowned for her superb birthday and wedding cakes. It was so beautifully decorated it seemed a shame to cut it.

This was, indeed, a birthday to remember. As it turned out to be, but perhaps not in the way everyone expected.

At another party, Carol Sutton was in the middle of a pleasant conversation with Beth Reed, a friend from University days, when Simon, his sun-streaked blond head held high, strode up to them. Without a preliminary word, he broke rudely into the conversation, laying a firm hand on Carol's shoulder. "We have to get a start right now," he said in his arrogant fashion.

Beth, who didn't like Simon Mansfield one little bit and couldn't for the life of her see why her friend Carol would, took him on. "Get started where? I thought you were enjoying the party?" It was a good party. No one had left so far.

"We have another party to attend," Simon said, dislike in his voice.

"Really? Which one?" Beth looked him in the eye.

"My cousin's, of course." His expression also showed a degree of exasperation. He hated being challenged by women. He didn't see females as his equal. "You know of her. Everyone does. Charlotte Mansfield."

"Charlotte Mansfield? Big time!" Beth crowed. "People really admire her, you know. Especially us girls. She has the makings of a leader. Rumour has it you weren't invited to her party, Simon. You screwed up somehow or other."

Beside her outspoken friend, Carol was near hyperventilating. A surefire method to make Simon angry was to cross him. Her father was like that. Simon's expression was full of loathing of her friend.

Simon Mansfield was, without doubt, a handsome man, rich to boot, but no prize in the matrimony department, Beth thought. He was a prig and a controller. "A slight disagreement." He brushed off Beth's offensive words. "No more. Nothing came of it. We can't stand around chatting, Carol. We have to go."

"You're not driving up the mountain, surely?" Beth asked, suddenly concerned for the safety of her friend. Carol had been born late in life to her well-respected, dignified parents, now in their mid-sixties. Consequently Carol had lived a very quiet, overtly protected life. Until she met Simon Mansfield, that was. From that moment, Carol was doomed. Simon Mansfield had simply taken her over like a modern-day Svengali. Their unlikely romance had flourished, to the consternation of Carol's friends.

"I can't see how that's any of your business," Simon was saying, bringing Beth back to the moment, "but I assure you, I'm under the limit. Last call, Carol. Are you coming with me or not?"

Anxiety cast a shadow over Carol's face. "Ahm..." she murmured. Remarkably, Carol was dithering. Beth touched her arm to give her support. "If you're nervous, Carol, I'd advise you to stay here. It's getting late to be driving another ninety minutes or so to the Blue Mountains."

Once more Simon placed a heavy hand on Carol's thin shoulder. "It's hardly the Matterhorn," he scoffed. "You've said your piece, Ms. Reed. I'll take very good care of Carol, but thank you so much for your concern. Come along, Carol."

Carol was looking extremely upset. Why didn't she tell Mansfield to bugger off? Carol's friends would rally around. "You've certainly got a bullying way about you," Beth said, realizing she loathed this guy as much as he apparently loathed her. Simon Mansfield really needed to get himself sorted.

"And you should learn to mind your own business," Simon snapped, the colour rising to his lean cheeks.

Carol barely had time to say good night to her friend, let alone beg Beth to make her apologies to her hosts, before Simon moved her off so fast her feet were barely touching the ground. "What a truly detestable bitch," Simon gave his considered opinion of Beth Reed. "I've always thought she was gay," he said with sweeping intolerance.

"She *isn't*," Carol found the courage to reply. "As if anyone cares one way or the other. Beth is my friend."

Chapter 5

Royce Weld, Brendon's longtime close friend, was passing through the entrance hall in time to witness the unexpected arrival of Simon Mansfield. He had a rather plain young woman glued to his side. Royce knew Mansfield hadn't been invited, so he made a dash to Brendon's side, pulling him away from the laughing group that circled him.

"Bren, I say—guess who's here?"

Brendon turned to give Royce his full attention. "Santa?" he asked, with a deadpan face.

"Try again. The insufferable Simon Mansfield. He has some poor girl in tow. She doesn't look happy."

"My God!" Instantly Brendon felt his temper rise. "What a bloody nuisance! Where is he?"

"He was coming through the door when I spotted him. I believe he was about to place Charlie's birthday present under the tree," Royce said.

"Was he now?" Brendon said grimly. "I might have to enlist your aid to run him back to his car."

"No problem. I suppose Charlie should be told? Hang on, here she comes," he said in relief. "She's got a real antennae for trouble, has Charlie. Might be best we go softly . . . softly."

"I'm not buying that, Royce. I *know* Mansfield. The way I see it is he's here to make trouble."

"I get the picture. So, what now?"

"We have a word—" Brendon broke off as Charlotte, moving like a gazelle, reached them.

"What's up?" She looked from Bren to their friend Royce. Even as she said it, she *knew.* "Don't tell me. Simon has turned up like the proverbial bad penny?"

"He wants aggro. He'll get aggro," Brendon bit off. "Royce and I will escort him back to his car."

"Is Carol with him?" Charlotte asked.

"A plain girl? Well, sort of plain, a bit dreary, but *nice?*" Royce asked. "Not Simon's usual companion, that's for sure. Mansfield is said to be smart, but I always thought he was pretty thick."

"Don't let's turn this into a major incident," Charlotte said, thinking fast. "Leastways not yet. Not until we absolutely have to. I'll go greet them. Act as if we were expecting them. I like Carol. I don't think she's had an easy life."

"Yeah, in a convent?" quipped Royce.

"I'll come with you," Brendon said.

"No, you won't. Please, Bren." Charlotte put her hand on his arm. "You're like a red flag to a bull so far as Simon is concerned. I can handle him. Royce can come with me. He doesn't have a black belt."

"Just another one of Bren's skills," said Royce, so admiring of his friend. Brendon was superbly fit. He worked at it.

"There's no easy ride with your cousin, Charlotte," Brendon warned. "He hates you. Therefore he has to be watched." He didn't add that there were minders out there keeping track of the evening's events. But no one had told them to bar Simon Mansfield from the party. He was, after all, a member of the family.

Royce took a deep breath, feeling like he had wandered onto a minefield. Unlike Brendon, he wasn't equipped to dance with danger. "I'll come get you if we need you, Bren," he said, fully intending to act on his promise. Privately he thought Mansfield could be a bit of a nutter. The rich seemed to have the idea they were somehow above the law. Charlie and Bren aside, that was.

Charlotte gave her cousin a brilliant smile, mindful of the small curious crowd around the tree. She took a few steps forward to acknowledge Carol with a kiss on the cheek. "I was beginning to think you'd never turn up."

Carol's frantic heartbeat slowed. Simon answered for both of them. "Wouldn't miss your party for the world," he cried. "We had to see the Cornells first. The tree looks splendid, Charlotte. Happy birthday, by the way. Your present is the one with the emerald and red bow."

"Why, thank you. I did say not to bother with presents, but no one was listening," Charlotte responded, grateful the temperature in the entrance hall had dropped a few points. "Come on through. The buffet is still open."

"That'd be great!" Simon was affability itself. Seized again by the arm, Carol permitted herself a small, relieved smile. Charlotte looked glorious, she thought. A golden girl and so *kind*. She had been praying right through the trip to Clouds. She hoped with all her heart that God had listened. Not that He always did, in her experience. Inside the living room a seriously good group of musicians was playing a medley of popular tunes.

Back in the living room, Charlotte watched her cousin amble up to a group who knew him. Nobody appeared in a rush to greet him, but after a minute or two, with Simon on his best behaviour and his girlfriend so obviously nice and refined, everyone settled.

"Well then?" Charlotte waited for Brendon's response.

Brendon drew a quick, hard breath. "I don't trust him, Charlotte. He's going to string everyone along and then he's going to let fly. You took the wrong course. Royce and I could have ejected him."

"What else could I do?" Charlotte's eyes were sparking. "He brings Carol along like some kind of hostage."

"What's wrong with the girl?" Brendon wanted to know. "It's beyond strange. How can she be so stupid?"

"She thinks she loves him, Bren."

"Then she's soft in the head."

"Sometimes feeling sways reason. She's desperate for love," Charlotte pointed out with compassion.

"She won't get it from your cousin," Brendon returned. "She'll finish up a damaged woman. Damn it, this is your birthday party, Charlie. Everything was going so well."

Charlotte shook his arm. "Don't worry. Worse comes to worst, you do have your black belt."

He shook his handsome head. "I'm sorry, Charlotte," he said. "Sorry. Sorry. Sorry."

"It's okay, Bren." Momentarily she leaned against him, drawing strength from his body, which she felt was *perfect*. "It's *my* family. I have to deal with them. I pretty much knew Simon would turn up.

Maybe his darling mother egged him on. It helps if Aunt Patricia comes out in the open. She's been undercover for far too long."

"She's actually your *enemy*, Charlotte," he said sombrely.

Charlotte was searching her memory. "She would have been very happy to make trouble for my mother. Funny thing about jealousy is that it does away with conscience. Anyway, I'm not going to stand around waiting for Simon to accuse me of stealing the family fortune. I'm going to dance."

"Just as well I'm available," said Brendon, in a smooth, dry voice. His suddenly smiling silver-grey eyes were back on hers. She felt the twist of her heart. He put one arm around her waist, leading her back to the dance floor. Brendon was determined to keep a close protective watch on Charlotte. It was part of who he was.

Simon took well over an hour before he launched his attack. He had waited so he could get in some of the sumptuous buffet, accompanied by a few drinks. He truly believed he was in the right. The birthday girl was at the heart of the Mansfield family's huge problem. She had stolen the family fortune right from under his father's nose. It was the biggest heist on family record. His head and his veins were thrumming with an altogether manic outrage. He could think of no good reason not to spoil her lavish birthday party. God only knew what she was wearing around her neck! He had never seen it before. It must have cost tens of thousands of dollars.

She was standing at the edge of the dance floor. Needless to say, Macmillan was right beside her. They looked so eye-catching together, no one could look anywhere else. Of course Macmillan was going after the heiress in his smooth, ruthless fashion. His family would be backing him. Good old Brendon Macmillan. He had been waiting for ages to snaffle up the little heiress. That they looked so *right* together only served to increase his rage. It would be a positive joy to embarrass them in front of their friends.

Carol, her face blanched white, had sensed his intent. She gave him such a look of entreaty it almost brought him to his senses. Instead, he physically thrust her away. As he began to move towards them, he saw Macmillan turn Charlotte into his arms.

"That's it, dance with the little heiress, Macmillan," he called in a challenging voice. "You do that. What are you going to do with her afterwards? Pick her up, throw her on a bed, and shag her senseless, you big, macho guy?" His tanned skin began to blotch as he abandoned himself to a near-orgasmic rage. It gave him a feeling of power he never felt otherwise. "Promise her you're going to spend the rest of your life making her happy. God knows you'll have your hands on her money."

It was a dreadful moment. Strangely enough, no one was truly aghast except possibly Mansfield's girlfriend, Carol, who looked like she was about to faint.

Simon swung his head quickly to harangue the guests. "You all know it, don't you? He's after her. He always was. He's after the money. The Macmillans can't get enough. She robbed us, you know. She robbed my father, the rightful heir. She robbed . . ."

There it was again, the same old litany. Brendon didn't plan on waiting for the rest. He moved like a big cat towards Charlotte's insufferable cousin, seeing out of the corner of his eye Carol Sutton bursting into tears.

"Never mind him. Never mind him, Brendon." Charlotte went after Brendon, dragging on his arm. She knew Brendon would flatten her cousin for sure. Even the way he was moving put her in mind of a jungle cat ready to pounce.

Only that didn't happen. Two tall, heavily built men wearing dark suits suddenly appeared as if by magic. They went to either side of Simon, who had stiffened in shock, got a firm hold on him, then began bearing his slumped form backwards. Simon's large feet were dragging on the floor as he tried in vain to find purchase. Rage wasn't drowning him. It was humiliation. They were out of the living room and into the entrance hall, with Simon protesting all the while.

After the terrible moment of shock, it suddenly seemed funny. Who were those guys, the Blues Brothers? They could hear Simon continuing to protest at the top of his lungs, ready to yell "police brutality" but clearly unable to identify who the men were. There would have been a lot of crowd satisfaction in seeing Brendon knock Mansfield flat, but this was a tidier outcome. Most guessed the two men had been hired for the evening as security guards. They must have been alerted, as indeed they had been by one Royce Weld, who sought to protect his dear friends.

By 2 a.m. the guests bound for Blue Horizons motel were taken there by a specially chartered bus. The remainder of the guests who were staying over at the house had retired, happily exhausted. Breakfast would be served from 8:30 a.m. onward for those who could make it, lunch at 1 p.m. for those who liked to sleep it off. It had been a marvellously entertaining night. Simon Mansfield, well over the limit, had not been allowed to drive his car. His keys had been withheld. A small room not up to his usual standard had been found for him at the motel. Charlotte hadn't had much difficulty persuading Carol Sutton to stay on at Clouds. The two people who were left standing were Charlotte, the birthday girl, and Brendon, who was going around the huge house turning off lights. When he returned through the house, he found Charlotte standing outside her uncle's study. One hand was on the brass handle of the door.

"I was wondering when you'd decide to take a peek," he said. "You'll have wonderful luck if you find it open."

"You're so right," Charlotte muttered. "He really shouldn't have done that."

Brendon sighed. "Charlotte, you've allowed them far too much licence. They think the house is theirs."

She answered with a sigh of her own. "I really didn't want to kick them out. Conrad is my uncle. He's a distinguished novelist. I understand perfectly how Clouds suits him."

"And it saves him having to buy a suitable retreat for himself," Brendon pointed out. "There are other beautiful houses here in the mountains with outstanding views."

"Clouds would be the pick of them. And there's the garden. He would see his mother moving around in the garden, wouldn't he? Everyone loved Grandma."

Brendon touched her gently on her shoulder, bare except for a shoestring strap. A gesture he had made countless times, yet now it was *different.* "They have to go, Charlotte." His hand didn't linger. It burned. "You must let them go. However forgiving you are, your uncle and aunt have treated you very badly. And Simon is a disgrace."

"He's close to paranoid," Charlotte said. "Anyway, I can get in here. I know where the spare key is."

Brendon looked down at her in wry amusement. "Charlie, most probably it has been shifted. It's been years!"

"This was Daddy's study, you know. Uncle Conrad took it over. He wouldn't know where the spare key is hidden. Only me."

"And me, I hope?" His voice held more than a hint of challenge.

"You've earned it. Follow me."

Brendon shook his head. "Charlotte, there simply aren't words to match my relief at your faith in me," he drawled.

She led him back into the entrance hall, moving past the glittering Christmas tree to the gilt-wood console table. It was surmounted by a tall, elegant gilt-wood mirror with a carved crest.

"Should I guess?" Brendon asked, his eyes ranging over both antiques.

"Go right ahead," she invited.

"Not the mirror," he concluded. "Too high for a little girl. The console here, maybe. God knows there are enough scrolls and swags and things. If anywhere, I'd say the central mask." He bent closer.

"Nice one," Charlotte said. "It *is* the mask, but which bit do you press?"

"What do you say *you* do it?" he said. "It's nearly three o'clock in the morning."

"So what? I'm wide awake. So are you, by the look of it. If someone else has beaten me to it, I'm seriously you-know-what." Making a little tent with her slender fingers, Charlotte found a point on the head of the winged female grotesque. She pressed it with her forefinger. "Voilà!" A square box popped out of the ornate gilt-wood scroll at the base of the mask. "God bless my dear father for telling me," Charlotte breathed.

"God bless him, indeed." Brendon was impressed.

"Now, to the study. There's a safe in there," Charlotte said. "It used to be behind a Brett Whiteley." She named a very famous Australian artist.

"Don't tell me. You know the combination?"

"Yes, I do," Charlotte breathed. "I was always good with numbers, even as a kid."

"Not only are you beautiful, but you are also intellectually gifted, dear girl."

The brass key Charlotte had extracted from the console's central scroll slid into place. With a single turn it unlocked the study door. Brendon found the lights panel inside. The spacious room with its air of privilege and substance sprang to life.

"Much as it used to be," Charlotte said, with a sad tug on her heart. She could *see* her father and her grandfather seated behind the twin pedestal partners' desk. She had loved the terrestrial and celestial globes that adorned the room when she was a child. Both her father and her grandfather had been highly pleased by her interest in them. Both had enjoyed pointing out all the countries of the world and the planets. She looked towards the wall to her left. "The Whiteley is still in place. The safe is behind it."

A kind of acceptance of everything she did settled into Brendon. "You mean to open it?"

"Just to take a peek. Legally speaking, this is *my* safe. All I want is to sight a nice, thick manuscript. I won't attempt to read it."

Brendon went behind the burr-walnut partners' desk. It had four short and two long drawers to each side. He tried them. "I can't think why not. The drawers are locked, as well," he announced, unsurprised. "What the heck has he got in there?"

"Maybe nothing," Charlotte replied with a shrug. "He'd be as anxious to hide nothing as anything. If there is a manuscript, as Aunt Patricia claimed, it will be in the safe, wouldn't you say? He wouldn't have taken it into town with him. They'll be back tonight."

"By which time Simon might be fit enough to take off," Brendon said crisply. He stood watching, while Charlotte, the safe cracker, went to work. Twenty-one years old and she had an arsenal of talents, he thought in amusement.

The door of the safe opened, when he'd been a tiny bit afraid it wouldn't. Immediately Charlotte's hand shot out, delving inside. "Half a dozen jewellery boxes, lots of private papers, files," she reported, then she said, "For crying out loud." She turned her head to look at Brendon. "No manuscript!"

"If you were to ask my opinion, there *is* no manuscript," Brendon said. "I don't suppose it's uncommon, but your uncle might have written himself out with *Cries of the Heart*. He mightn't have had it in him to write a follow-up. Maybe he had writer's block."

Charlotte shook her head. "Except real writers *write*. Something in them compels them to do it. My father wrote. He once said he had a good novel in him. I write, not a wonderful novel like Uncle Conrad, but we committed writers need to commit ourselves to paper, our thoughts, our dreams, our full quota of unhappy times, family tragedies. *Cries of the Heart* seemed to me more than a little autobiographical. It was the story, a love story, of a highly dysfunctional, yet wealthy family. Actually, it was my father who coined the phrase

'*Cries of the Heart*,' not Uncle Conrad. He never did own up to pinching it. It was a splendid line, too good not to use. Did you try the bookcases?"

"If there is a manuscript, it wouldn't be in any place on show."

"I guess not. When Daddy was overseas, he wrote me long letters brimming with life. I loved them. I kept them. I always answered, my heart yearning for him to come home. I have to say I was my father's daughter more than my mother's daughter. It wasn't intentional. It was just the way it was. If my father had lived long enough, I'm sure he would have written a novel to even surpass *Cries of the Heart*."

Brendon stared at her, his voice curiously edgy. "There's the big question, of course."

"Come out with it."

"Your *father* could have written *Cries of the Heart*, not your uncle," he suggested as the notion sprang into his mind. "A manuscript could well have existed, written by your father, which your uncle found after your father's death," he further expounded. "Everyone knew Conrad, like Christopher, had artistic leanings."

Charlotte experienced another moment of déjà vu. "You mean, after Uncle Conrad dried his crocodile tears, he took another long look at the manuscript he'd found and fancied himself as the author?" Whatever memory had come to mind, it slipped away. "Even I don't think Uncle Conrad is as bad as that," she said. "It wouldn't just be plagiarism. It would be a crime."

"Definitely. You could always plead with him to let you read the manuscript for his current novel. After all, you've allowed him to stay at Clouds for years now to plan, and then write, the next masterpiece. It must exist if Patricia has been allowed to read it."

"I don't believe her," Charlotte answered. "I feel very sad in here. I remember the old life."

Brendon saw clearly that she was distressed. "Let's go to bed," he said, briskly.

Charlotte laughed out loud. "You're kidding. You can't have your wicked way with me, Brendon Macmillan."

"Who said I wanted to?" he instantly replied.

"Simon did. He said, if you recall, you fully intended at some time in the near future to shag me senseless?"

"As he so charmingly put it," Brendon reacted with disgust. "He really is despicable."

"I agree. Anyway, you may have your many adoring girlfriends, but you're pretty straitlaced with me."

"I should damned well think so," Brendon retorted. "I'm turning the lights off, so move. What I should have said was, *Let's go upstairs.*"

"You sound almost angry?" Charlotte asked, as she stepped into the corridor.

"I will be in a minute. Take off those silly shoes."

"They're not silly shoes!" she protested, staring down at them. "They're Valentino."

"I can't guess at what these male designers are thinking, turning out shoes with heels so thin and high women could break their necks."

Charlotte bent to remove the offending evening sandals. "Well, top models have been known to crash on the runways. Anyway, shows how good I am. We won the tango, thanks to me."

"That's odd. Lisa told me *I* stole the show."

"She would. She's madly in love with you, Bren. You hold her heart in your hands."

"And I'm sorry about that," he said. "I gave Lisa no good reason for her high hopes."

Charlotte gave a poignant smile. "*La coeur a ses raisons qui la raison ne connait point.*"

He was moved by the words and her low-pitched, musical voice. "You speak French well."

"I figure it had something to do with having a great French-born teacher. Anyway, it held up in Paris." As she went to lead the way, Brendon shocked her with a single movement. He swept her off her feet. She might have been a bundle of feathers so high did he hold her in his arms. "What is this, a replay of *Gone With the Wind*?" she gasped.

He glanced down at her flushed, excited face. "Charlie, you're in reach and yet you're out of reach."

"No matter what your family wants?"

He didn't answer that provocation. He proceeded to carry her up the stairs and along the silent corridor of the west wing. He put her down gently, right outside her door. With one hand, he opened it, and then turned to leave. "Get some sleep, Charlie. It'll be another big day tomorrow."

She caught his sleeve, her beautiful green eyes sparkling with mischief and something that was no laughing matter. "I won't say no to a good-night kiss. I'm twenty-one, remember?"

He swung back, his handsome face taut and unsmiling. "Don't think you can twist me around your little finger," he warned.

"You think I can't?" she asked in a veiled whisper.

The sheer beauty of her caused him acute tension. "Come here, then."

Of a sudden, emotion overwhelmed her. She had thrown down the gauntlet, and Bren had picked it up. This was the Brendon she had known all her life, yet he was shocking her thoroughly, forcing her to face a hitherto unexplored fact. She was in love with him. She would be a perfect fool if she couldn't now see that. She was literally shaking with need of him. It was Brendon whom she wanted. She always had. She knew what his family wanted. Did Brendon want that, too? Would she ever fight free of their powerful influence? She made a little sound, almost a mew of pain, at her own vulnerability.

Brendon stifled it with his mouth. He pulled her slight, girlish body tight against his tall frame, aware he had cut off her little sob. Without qualm, without another single coherent thought, he grasped a handful of her curling golden mane, tilting her head back so he could better claim her mouth. It was utter, utter rapture. One of those times when a man was frantic to tear off his clothes to know the nakedness of the woman he so hotly desired.

Only this was Charlotte shaking under his hands.

He wrenched back his head, afraid he couldn't control the highly combustible situation. "Charlie," he said, raggedly, "the surest way for us to derail our lives is for this to go any further."

For answer, Charlotte buried her face against his shirtfront, taking deep, deep breaths. "I understand, Bren. I provoked you," she said at length.

"Everything is okay. Truly." He kissed the top of her head. "What we are going to do is give you space. You're going to need it. From now on in, you'll have a tremendous amount of clout as Sir Reginald's heir. Clever as you are, there will be so much to learn. You know that. So many people you have to get onside. Not just family, people inside the firm. You've started out in brilliant fashion, but there are greatly experienced QCs in Chambers, not the least of them my father. There are going to be those who resent you, even those ready to oppose you. Many things have to be settled, not only in your life, but mine. You're going to find any number of men who will want to marry you. They won't just be after your money, Charlotte, believe me. They'll be after *you*. *You* without a penny to your name would be a lifetime prize."

"I can handle them," Charlotte said, staunchly, when there was no real way of knowing whether she could. It was Bren she feared she couldn't handle. She intended to keep that to herself as a means of self-protection, self-autonomy. Besides, as usual, Bren was right. There were countless *huge* hurdles facing her. Problems that had to be solved. She took a determined little step away from him, knowing she had to go to earth with her deepest emotions. At least for some time. "See you in the morning," she said in a near-normal voice. "I loved my birthday party, Bren."

"Just wait until you open all the presents," he said, grateful the tumult inside him was gradually winding down.

Charlotte hardly had a moment to herself for the entire day. She had appeared at breakfast, which was sparsely attended, then again at lunch, when all her guests turned up. Afterwards everyone had assembled in the entrance hall while all her presents were opened. Brendon and Lisa helped out. She hadn't wanted her guests to spend money on her—indeed, she had asked them not to—but no birthday party guest ever takes notice of that. The presents were beautiful, expensive. Silver, boxes, vases, bowls, crystal glassware, ornaments, adornments, small gems of flower paintings that she loved. Brendon's gift was an exquisite nineteenth-century Blanc de Chine Guanyin. The goddess stood on a gleaming wood base, her long hair scrolling across her shoulders much in the manner Charlotte often wore her hair, as Brendon later pointed out. It was a gift Charlotte knew she would treasure to her dying day.

It was now late afternoon, and Charlotte and Brendon were waiting none too patiently for her uncle and aunt to return from Sydney. The fact that their son had not been invited to Charlotte's party had clearly bothered them. That their son might well bother Charlotte had apparently not been a cause of concern. The present Simon had left beneath the Christmas tree was a papier-mâché desk stand inlaid with mother of pearl. She had seen it somewhere before, many years ago, possibly in her grandfather's study. She prided herself on her good memory.

Charlotte's uncle and aunt finally arrived home towards dusk. Charlotte and Brendon did not go out to greet them. They waited in front of the glittering Christmas tree for the hazardous moment when the Mansfields would join them.

Conrad Mansfield came through the front door, dragging a small suitcase. He was the first one to speak, his handsome face showing his displeasure, his brows beetled. "You really needn't have waited," he said.

"It seems to me, Uncle, I can pick my times. I expect you've heard from Simon?"

Before her uncle could answer, Patricia Mansfield moved into the entrance hall. She too appeared displeased. She set down a small case before pushing in front of her husband, every inch the indignant, possessive mother. "Simon claims he was manhandled?" she fired back.

To everyone's surprise, her husband rounded on her, with a face of thunder. "Forget all that, Patricia," he exclaimed. "I expect Simon got what he deserved. You ruined our boy. He'll never become a man with you around."

Patricia Mansfield looked her fury at having private family matters aired. "You might add, 'for want of a proper father,' " she struck back, clearly out for revenge.

Charlotte judged it time to intervene. "If you need to have a frank talk, may I ask that you do it in private?" she suggested. "We really stayed on because I have a question to ask, Uncle Conrad. I never talk about rights—*my* rights—but I've allowed you to stay at Clouds for some years now in order to write your next book."

"So?"

Something in the coldness of his expression sent a chill through her. She was beginning to feel her own uncle was a danger to her. "So, you've hardly shown your appreciation."

"*You* have no interest in Clouds," he said, as though she was being ridiculous.

"Then you have no real knowledge of me, Uncle. You've never shown any interest in me. You never made me, your niece, your brother's only child, feel cared for, certainly not loved. Obviously you don't understand me at all. I love Clouds. Grandpa recognized that, that's why he left it to me."

"You mean, he left you the *lot!*" Patricia Mansfield burst out, as though wishing Charlotte could finally get the unfairness of it straight.

"Why don't you leave us, Aunt Patricia?" Charlotte said, sick to death of all the talk of money and being robbed. "It's my uncle I wish to speak to."

"About what?" Conrad condescended to ask. The collar of his casual blue-and-white-checkered shirt was open, revealing surprisingly part of a tattoo.

That surprised Charlotte. A tattoo? She looked to Brendon, who gave her a nod to continue. She wanted Brendon there as her best friend and as a superbly fit young man. Her uncle and aunt were trying to intimidate her, at the very least. "About your new book," she said. "Aunt Patricia told me she had read the manuscript. I'm not asking to read it—you may not be ready for that—but I do want to see the finished pages."

"Whatever for?" demanded Patricia, as though Charlotte was proposing to bend rules that were written in stone.

"Because I can't wait to sight it," Charlotte replied. "To retain the privilege of staying on here, I need to be certain there *is* a book."

"*Wh-a-t?*" Patricia Mansfield spoke so loudly she let out all the air in her lungs. She waved a scornful hand. "Put her in her place, Conrad, why don't you?" she managed hoarsely.

Conrad Mansfield gave an odd smile. "I very much doubt I can. Charlotte might be a mere slip of a girl, but she's tough. It's in the blood."

"Balls!" Patricia shouted crudely. It was clear her husband wasn't about to back her, so she turned on her heel, making for the stairs. "I won't be seeing you again this evening, so I'll say good night." Her furious eyes ranged over Charlotte and Brendon, tall and formidable beside her.

"Good night, Aunt Patricia. With all due respect, I suggest you reevaluate your position here," Charlotte said. "You resent it, I know, but Clouds does belong to *me*. I have the authority to say who lives or does not live here."

Patricia's hand on the banister revealed her white knuckles. "You're like your mother, Charlotte. You're missing a heart."

From chill to burn. "The person missing a heart, Aunt Patricia, is *you*."

"Perhaps we could go into the study, sir?" Brendon suggested.

Conrad Mansfield gave the much younger man a bitter smile. "I read you as a young man destined to get to the very top, Brendon. My father, who never felt pride in me, actually admired you even as a boy. He used to call you the Macmillan panther."

"I have heard that. I don't know why."

"I think you do. I daresay you've been under massive pressure all your life to make your family proud. Many a young man would have gone under, gotten into drugs, the playboy lifestyle, whatever. You had a lot of guts to call on. Just like Charlotte here. I'm absolutely certain your family, including you, are working to take my niece over. Possibly even lure her into marriage."

Charlotte cut in. "Marriage is a long way off, Uncle Conrad. I've only just turned twenty-one. I'll be called on to step into my grandfather's shoes or hand over the reins to someone far better qualified. I don't intend to be taken over at any price, but we're avoiding this issue of your new book. I appreciate that *Cries of the Heart* is a hard act to follow, but you must have something to show after all this time?"

His frown deepening, Conrad Mansfield stared down his straight nose at his niece. "You're a writer . . . of sorts," he said condescendingly. "Your father used to let me read your letters. He was so proud of you and the fact that you were so clever, a little girl full of such vitality and energy, with a marvellous appreciation of language." Conrad turned to make his way to the study. "Come along then," he invited. "It's by no means finished. A project like this takes time. Years if it has to."

"Your publisher hasn't asked for a definite date?" Brendon asked.

"Maybe there never will be one," Conrad Mansfield muttered, almost beneath his breath.

"You're saying this book may never be finished?" Brendon followed up the muffled comment.

"Plenty of books are never finished," Mansfield said.

Outside the study door, he produced a key from his pocket. "I usually lock the study when I'm away."

Charlotte shot Brendon a sidelong glance. "I know there's a spare somewhere."

Her uncle paused to stare at her. "There *was* one. I've never found it."

"Is there the need for such secrecy?" Charlotte asked.

"I have my reasons," he replied. "Now, I'll allow you to hold the manuscript in your hand, Charlotte. You told me you didn't want to read it before publication, so we'll hold to that, agreed?"

"Have you a working title?" Charlotte asked. "I believe *Cries of the Heart* was a phrase you borrowed from my father?"

Conrad Mansfield, who had been moving towards the wall of bookcases, swung back so abruptly his long white ponytail flipped around his throat like a rope. For a split second, he appeared acutely disturbed. There were deep grooves between his eyes. "My dear girl, wherever did you get that idea?" He wagged an admonishing finger.

"Directly from my father," Charlotte promptly replied. "My mother had left for Sydney, I remember. My parents had had an argument. I overheard it. When my father realized, he hugged me close. I remember exactly what he said to me: '*Cries of the heart, my darling. Cries of the heart.*' "

Conrad Mansfield stared back at Charlotte as though he could scarcely credit what she was saying. "You seem very certain of this?"

"I remember that moment very clearly. A lot I can't remember at all. Some things are coming back. Resurfacing, I could say. I was badly traumatized after the death of my parents."

"Of course you were, my dear. We all were. The Mercedes scattered all over the valley floor. They had to have been arguing violently. That was the only explanation. It was a time of madness for us all. My father turned into a coldhearted monster. My poor mother—Christopher and I knew perfectly well she had always been unhappy with my father—just gave up, took a leave of absence on life. Christopher was her favourite. Christopher was everyone's favourite. I was smart enough, good-looking enough, yet the best I could be was Chris's shadow."

"But you wrote a masterpiece," Brendon reminded him, watching Conrad Mansfield closely.

"I beg your pardon?" Conrad asked blankly, like he had lost all track of the conversation.

"A masterpiece. *Cries of the Heart*?" Brendon prompted.

"Yes, yes, of course." The blank expression lifted. "I didn't have any other choice if I was to impress my father. I should tell you,

Charlotte, the words '*cries of the heart*' were original to me. Chris would have heard me say it. Such words were appropriate to what was going on at the time."

"I'm sorry, Uncle, but I don't think that's true," Charlotte flatly contradicted him.

"My dear child, I assure you it *is*." Conrad Mansfield appeared flabbergasted by her response. "Your father didn't write *Cries of the Heart*. I did."

"*I* didn't claim my father wrote *your book*," Charlotte said. "I only said he gave you the title. Please may I see the manuscript now?"

"As a special concession, Charlotte, you may."

"It's a wonder you didn't put it in the safe," Charlotte said, catching Brendon's silver warning look a second too late.

Conrad Mansfield gave an uncontrollable groan. "You remember the safe?" His voice contained anger and a good dash of anxiety.

"Of course I do." Charlotte was sufficiently alert not to mention she knew the safe's combination.

"Too hard to remember the combination?" her uncle asked, his lips curled. Of course she couldn't. She had been a child, though he didn't doubt his brother might have told her.

Charlotte shrugged. "I was too young."

"Of course, though I wouldn't have been surprised if my father or Christopher showed you. You were only a child, but a very inquisitive child, as I recall. The safe is where, do you remember?"

Her uncle was eyeing her in a way that Charlotte found truly disturbing. She knew she was being tested. "Behind the Brett Whiteley, over there." She gestured at the iconic painting of Sydney Harbour.

"Aren't you a clever girl!" he said, with a cold smile on his face.

"I'm supposed to be, remember? In the blood?"

Brendon once again thought it wise to intervene. He could sense a kind of desperation about Conrad Mansfield. He also sensed violence flexing in the man. "If you could let us see the manuscript, sir, we can go on our way. It's been a long day."

"My niece may hold it, not you, Brendon. You're not family. At least not *yet*."

Brendon's silver-grey eyes flashed. "I don't recommend you keep up that insinuation, sir. Nor do I recommend you start any gossip rolling."

Conrad Mansfield's malicious expression was wiped clean. "My lips are sealed, dear boy."

Brendon forced himself not to say, "*I'm not your dear boy.*" He and Charlotte watched as Conrad Mansfield walked to the section of the bookcase nearest the partners' desk. He pulled out a few weighty leather-bound, gold-tooled tomes, placed them on the desk, and then withdrew a substantial pile of papers that had been placed inside a manila folder.

"You've done a generous amount of work then?" Charlotte said, putting out her hands to take the hefty document.

"It's a long story," her uncle said. "I don't blame you for wanting to see it. I'm oversensitive about it, afraid it won't rate when compared with the first book. That does happen. Patricia, of course, is adamant I finish it."

Charlotte looked down at the thick folder. There had to be nearly a ream of paper there. "I would love to read it," she said.

At that, Conrad Mansfield moved to take the manuscript off her. "And so you shall—when it's finished."

"I do hope you will allow me to read the first page at least," Charlotte said, not about to hand the file over. Did he really think she would?

"Why are you so hard to convince?" her uncle asked, endeavouring to stare her down.

"What concerns you, sir?" Brendon asked. "Charlotte has only asked to see the first page. I would think you'd be only too pleased to let her read the rest. Charlotte, as you are aware, is a very gifted young woman. Feedback must be important to you?"

"All right then, go ahead!" Conrad cried. There were ragged edges to his whole persona.

"Thank you." Charlotte put the heavy folder down on the desktop, shifting her grandfather's antique silver inkstand to accommodate it. Something about this thick pile of papers spoke to her. She wanted to open the file. Found she couldn't. Her tapering fingers hovered several inches above it.

"Open it, Charlie," Brendon told her briskly, noting her hesitation.

"Leave the girl alone," Conrad Mansfield barked, turning on Brendon.

It seemed such an easy thing to do, yet Charlotte was continuing to hesitate. "Do you need help, Charlie?" Brendon asked, ignoring Conrad, who appeared to him to be on the verge of panic.

"Of course not. I was merely being reverential," Charlotte said, tongue-in-cheek.

There was no title page. No inscription. A trained speed reader, Charlotte took little time to read through and better yet, absorb the front page. She could hardly believe what she read. She couldn't even associate it with the author of *Cries of the Heart*. Opening lines, let alone the first page, had to draw in the reader. That was a given. Even for a first draft this wasn't good. In fact, it was embarrassingly bad. It appeared to be the start of a thriller? That much was apparent. Yet how could a man with such a gift write this? The text had been heavily annotated, underlined, asterisked, like an amateur's first attempt.

She shut the file quietly, wondering what in heaven's name she had learned. "Thank you, Uncle Conrad," she said, her level tone masking her shock. Was it possible her uncle had only one great book in him? Even so, he couldn't have written this, surely?

"Not bad, eh?" her uncle asked, looking immensely relieved.

"Difficult to tell without reading further," Brendon said, wondering why Charlotte hadn't seized her opportunity to at least riffle through the pages.

"You'll just have to wait for that." Conrad smirked behind his heavy moustache. Every trace of panic had gone out of his face.

They were in the car on their way back to Sydney before Charlotte found she could speak about what she had read. Her uncle had seen them off, back to his urbane self. "I'm sure you understand your aunt is upset about Simon," he said, patting Charlotte's shoulder like they were coconspirators. "I really should have been more of a hands-on parent, just as Patricia said. But then, I did have my book to get out."

"In a remarkably short time," Brendon slid in.

"It came easily, I admit. For far too long I've feared it was a stand-alone."

Charlotte couldn't find it within herself to make a comment. "We'll be in touch, Uncle Conrad," she said, giving little impression she was full of anger, regret, even pity.

"Drive safely now," he said, to all appearances the concerned loving uncle. He waited as Brendon shut the passenger door on Charlotte before walking around to the driver's side.

Conrad remained in place, waving them off. Charlotte couldn't bring herself to wave back. Instead she swallowed down an icy drip of alarm. She might not be able to remember, but intuitively she knew what her uncle was capable of. What both her uncle and aunt were capable of, for that matter, outwardly smiling, yet inwardly full of jealousy and years of banked-up resentments. One could conclude that would have happened early with her mother and father confirmed as Sir Reginald's "chosen ones." A barrier would always have been there. It didn't surprise her that her uncle had cast around frantically for some way to impress his father. That could have led him into willful and deliberate plagiarism.

"Well, what did you think?" Brendon broke the silence. They were clear of the estate and underway down the mountain. "Obviously even the opening page is going to need a lot of work?" he said, with a lick of black humour.

"Let's say it was a massive anticlimax." Charlotte sighed. "I feel sick even thinking about it."

"Not as bad as that, surely?" Brendon shot her a swift glance.

"A high school kid could do better," Charlotte told him, bleakly. "It's a thriller of some sort. Maybe even a detective story. It seems like it's going to be a total departure from *Cries of the Heart*, and it's certainly not going to turn the crime genre on its ear. God knows what the rest is all about, when the first page was so amateurish. I'd say Uncle Conrad is floundering badly."

"Even so, there appeared to be an entire manuscript there," Brendon pointed out. "You really should have demanded to read the lot, Charlie."

"Of course I should have," she said, her expression full of self-chastisement, "but believe it or not, I didn't want to embarrass him. If Aunt Patricia has read the manuscript, she must know whether it's good or not. She's no fool. The opening page needs to go into the trash. No true writer wrote it."

Brendon frowned. "So it's a puzzlement, unless your uncle didn't write *Cries of the Heart* at all." He was gradually coming to believe he had hit on the truth. "Your uncle found a manuscript tucked away in the study, read it, realized it was very good, and then decided to publish it as his own. Your father was dead. Your mother was dead. Your grandparents obviously knew nothing about a book that their son Christopher had written. Conrad thought he could get away with it."

"If you're right, he *has*," Charlotte confirmed, badly shaken. "What am I supposed to do," she asked, in near-despair, "have my uncle sued?"

"I don't suggest house detention." Brendon's answer was dry. "I can only repeat, you need to get them out of Clouds short of an eviction order. Hard to believe it, but they don't appreciate anything you've done for them, Charlie. Your uncle believes he has a perfect right to stay on. He is most likely hiding behind a massive lie."

"Only, proof isn't a single page. He could have been struggling with a genre that's new to him?"

"Charlie, babe, I don't accept that," Brendon groaned. "You don't love your uncle, and why would you? The thought that he could publish your father's book as his own leaves you stricken but loathe to expose him? I say he doesn't deserve your compassion. Obviously one can't *learn* to become a fine writer. One needs the gift. Conrad doesn't have it. Christopher did."

"I agree," Charlotte said quietly. "Only think of what he might do if I uncover him? His triumph exposed as a sham? He would want to punish me. He'd most likely want to kill me. Get someone else to do it, of course. I don't know what happened in the past, but something about Uncle Conrad makes me nervy, when I can't think of a single thing he ever did that would make me feel that way. We both know he pretty well ignored me."

Brendon extended a hand, giving her own hand a brief comforting pat. "You've always been very brave, Charlotte. It seems highly likely your uncle is a perfect fraud. He published a book that wasn't his own. Okay, we don't have *proof.* We're going on a gut instinct, our knowledge of the man, and your poor opinion of the opening page of the new opus, or so he says. Why don't you give them until into January to move out? That's a generous amount of time. Your uncle would have no difficulty finding another sanctuary in the Blue Mountains, as I've said before."

Charlotte looked through the darkened window up into the star-spangled, purplish-black night. They were almost at the site of her parents' fatal crash. It gave her the shudders. "It's all so bizarre, isn't it? But I suppose it's about time." Agitation was taking hold of her.

"I won't expose him. I can't. I can't expose the family. I'll just have to wait until my uncle dies. We both believe my father wrote *Cries of the Heart.* It was *his* personal triumph. It's my duty as his daughter to see that he is acknowledged the author—it's just not the right time."

"I should think you would want to vindicate your father," Brendon rasped. "Though I do see it would be difficult to take any other course of action right now. The scandal would rock both our families, members of Chambers who had been close friends with your father and know your uncle, the general public, the publishing house, and the critics. Of course, we're assuming your uncle's guilt, but his behaviour has tipped the balance—" Brendon broke off the conversation to take stock of what the car a short distance behind them was doing. The vehicle was moving too fast to safely negotiate the bends, he thought.

"What is it?" Charlotte was instantly alerted.

"Probably nothing." Brendon's eyes were blazing with concentration.

"For God's sake, what are they doing?" Charlotte cried, turning her head to look through the rear window. The car's headlights were dazzlingly bright. "They must be mad!" she said in alarm. "Even a total idiot wouldn't drive so recklessly, and on high beam. That's a danger to us."

"Seems more like they want a bloody race," Brendon gritted, moving his car farther to the right in case the lunatic behind them wanted to pass.

That seemed to be it. With considerable relief, they watched as the car that had been near tailgating them shot past at speed, compounding the driver's dangerous behaviour. A car could well have been coming up the mountain around the next bend. Once ahead of them, the vehicle braked dramatically, causing Brendon to sharply apply his own brakes.

"That can't be—That isn't that bloody fool Simon, is it?" he muttered, concerned that it could be.

Charlotte thought the same thing, but she was only too grateful the crisis had passed. "I don't recognize the number plate, but Simon does drive a BMW," she said. "There's a passenger in the car." They were close enough to see the outline of a woman's head. "I have the number plate now."

"Do you want to write it down? There's paper and pen in the glove box."

"No. I'll remember it," Charlotte said, confident she would. "It isn't a random bit of risky gamesmanship, is it? Some macho idiot who has had a drink too many and wanted to take on the Aston Martin?"

Brendon's eyes narrowed. "Whatever, I'm resolved to follow up the incident."

"Could it have been something symbolic?" Charlotte asked as the BMW moved farther and farther into the distance, with the driver continuing to disregard the speed limit.

"In what way?" Brendon asked, wondering if they were going to come across a bad accident ahead.

"My parents—?" Charlotte could go no further. She was trying to pull out of her vision of her father's car plunging off the road and into vast open space.

"Ah, Charlie!" Brendon sighed, getting that picture himself.

"Let me finish," Charlotte said. "Simon is a callous person. He's very quick to anger. It could well give him a sick pleasure to try to frighten us, to remind me in particular of the place of my parents' fatal crash."

"How could he have planned it?" Brendon asked, trying to crush the anger that rolled over him.

"He was in touch with his mother," Charlotte said. "He must have been in touch with Carol. We know Royce offered to give her a lift back to the city, but she appears so much under Simon's thumb she could have joined him at the motel. I'm sure she wasn't party to *that* stunt."

"I just don't know what to think about Carol," Brendon said. "At this point she appears brainwashed. If she has any sense at all, she'll get out of your cousin's life."

"Before it's too late," said Charlotte, thinking of the women who had done just that.

A fraught silence held between them. In making Charlotte his heiress, Sir Reginald had brought danger to her door, Brendon thought. Not from any madman who had a pathological hatred of the rich. The danger could well lie within her own family. Protecting Charlotte was going to be a full-time job. There was a real need to increase the watch on her. He would speak to both his grandfather and his father. He himself would have precious little free time. Pressure was on him to collect all the information his father and the QC needed for his cold case, an unsolved murder that had happened over twenty-five years before. New evidence had come to hand and all-important DNA testing had entered the game.

The atmosphere inside the speeding BMW was extraordinarily tense. "Are you trying to kill us, Simon?" Carol asked in a nerve-ridden voice. "Is that what you want?"

"Oh, do shut up," Simon snapped, suddenly banging the dash and further frightening Carol.

"We'll be picked up by the police, you know that." Carol had always been a law-abiding citizen, so she was aghast at Simon's reckless behaviour.

Simon only laughed. "It's Sunday evening. I know when to slow."

"They'll have your number plate," she warned him, hoping that would have some curbing effect.

Simon gave one of his overconfident laughs. "Our word against theirs," he said.

"You're expecting me to lie for you?" she asked in dismay.

He caught her hand, squeezed it *hard*. "Of course I do. You're my girl, aren't you?"

Carol shut her eyes, doing her best not to cry. How had things gone so bad so fast? "I don't like lying, Simon." He was pushing her. She had an unfamiliar urge to push back. "You could have caused a serious accident back there."

He threw her crushed hand back into her lap, the skin of his good-looking face pulled tight. "Nothing happened, did it? I know what I'm doing. I'm a great driver. It's another one of my talents. Macmillan will want to do something about it. First thing they'll do is check the registration. But you'll stand by me. Understand that?" He shot the slumped Carol a hard glance. "There's a lot you don't know about, Carol. A few things you do. What my grandfather did only brought harm to the family."

Carol dug deep to find some courage, though she knew it was

likely to escalate matters. "Well, you can't claim you were given a rough ride, Simon. To most people, you were left a massive sum of money."

It wasn't the answer Simon required. "The money is in a trust fund my grandfather set up," he snarled, shocked by her show of spirit. "He didn't think I'd be able to handle the money myself."

"Your grandfather would have wanted you to establish yourself," Carol suggested. "He would have wanted you to become an achiever."

"And I'm *not*? Is that what you're saying?" There was a deep frown on his face as he turned to her.

Carol very wisely backed off. Up until Charlotte's birthday party, it had not occurred to her that Simon Mansfield could be a danger. To his own cousin. To her. She had understood he had been angry and distressed that his father had been bypassed as Sir Reginald Mansfield's heir. She supposed any loving son would be. Now she understood the terrible anger that fired Simon up was all on his *own* account. Beth and other friends had confided their concerns about her involvement with Simon Mansfield. They had been highly critical of a young man who thought himself a "prince" and who lived way too high. Planted deep in Simon's psyche was the belief that he was better than everyone else. Now she saw she had foolishly involved herself with a narcissist—and a dangerous one at that. She felt shame. She knew her parents would be ashamed of her.

The huge problem facing her now was how to get out of this relationship. Simon certainly didn't love her. He probably lacked the capacity for loving, but he did regard her as a potential wife who would not dream of involving herself in his affairs, let alone going against him. She was well-bred, well-educated, reasonably good-looking. She was also efficient. Most people liked her. She would make a suitable hostess. Of course, once married she would have been expected to undergo a transformation in the matter of self-presentation: dress, hair, makeup, and so forth.

Carol sat straighter in the passenger seat. She wasn't going to lie for Simon Mansfield or anyone else. She had to hold fast to her principles. There were rules of conduct to be adhered to, rules that mattered. Simon might not love her, but he wouldn't take lightly any attempt on her part to break up. Her affections and hopes for a future together had dwindled to something approaching *fear.* She knew from what she had seen of him that Brendon Macmillan would go to hell and back to keep Charlotte safe. She would go beyond that: Brendon Macmillan was *in love* with Charlotte, whether he desired to be or not. All sorts of complications scored falling love with heiresses, she imagined. It was different for her. She had no one like that in her life. Things would probably get a lot worse before they got better. She knew that, but it was her chance to be unflinchingly brave.

Chapter 6

Brendon had to wait his turn to see his father, like everyone else. He wouldn't have wanted it any other way. However high he climbed, he was going to do it on merit. His opportunity came at the midmorning break.

"How's it going?" Julian Macmillan looked up smilingly from a pile of papers in front of him. He felt pleased to see the son he had been blessed with.

"Fine, Dad," Brendon said, taking a chair across the desk from his father. "It's not the Goldberg case. I'm on top of that. It's Simon Mansfield."

"Really?" Julian lifted his glasses off his nose and then rubbed the bridge. "Have you struck up an unlikely friendship?"

"Hardly."

"A very unpleasant young man, that. He was spoilt rotten by his doting mum, as you've heard any number of times. Conrad, who should have been a steadying influence, did nothing but write his book. Admittedly, it was a darn fine book."

Brendon decided to let his father in on his and Charlotte's suspicions. He explained all of their reasoning and concluded, "Charlotte and I don't think he wrote it."

Julian looked away across the spacious room, then back again. "Good God!" he murmured, quietly. "You want coffee?"

"Yes, please."

"Black, one sugar, just like me?"

"Thanks, Dad." He watched his father press a button, arranging for another cup to be brought in.

"You'll have to have some pretty convincing evidence," Julian warned.

"You don't sound all that shocked, Dad?"

"The truth will win out, won't it?" Julian said with a head shake.

"We don't have evidence that would hold up," Brendon admitted. "Charlotte asked if she could sight the manuscript. Patricia Mansfield told her she had read the opus so far."

"And?"

"It's like this." Brendon went on to recount what they had learned, breaking off momentarily as coffee arrived and was served.

"Thank you, Emily."

Emily smiled at both men and then left the room. "So it's only gut instinct you're going on," Julian Macmillan picked up on the conversation, not looking impressed.

"Okay, gut instinct," Brendon agreed, "but Charlotte said the opening page was so dismally bad it could not have been written by the author of *Cries of the Heart*."

"So on that flimsy basis, she thought her uncle had to have plagiarized what was her *father's* book? Is that it?"

"I'm delighted you hit on that, Dad. Charlotte is clever," he said, with quiet certainty.

"My God, yes," Julian breathed. "She's going to make a formidable woman. Not only that, a fascinating woman."

His father's smile seemed to Brendon to be a sad, knowing one. It prompted him to ask, "*Did* you have an affair with Charlotte's mother, Dad?" He had never doubted his father, unlike his mother, but there was something there. "I know you've always denied it, but I need to hear it again. I'm not standing in judgement, and I wouldn't dream of stirring up trouble, but I need the entire truth of the matter."

Julian Macmillan had no trouble looking his son in the eye. "There was *no* affair, Brendon," he said, no force but total honesty in his voice. "Alyssa was a very beautiful woman in all respects. A woman with a lot of power. I won't say I wasn't attracted to her. I *was*, no question about that. I won't lie to you. But then, so was just about every man who knew her, including the Old Man, who so favoured her. It wasn't just Alyssa's beauty, it was her personality, as well, her high intelligence. Christopher worshipped her. Christopher was strong, well able to stand up to his father, but he was also a sensitive man. An artistic man. To believe his wife had been unfaithful to him would have destroyed him."

"Well, he *was* destroyed, wasn't he? They both were. So who drove the knife home?" Brendon asked, his tone harsher than he intended. "Who tried to convince Christopher Mansfield her affair with you was true?"

"Do you really think I didn't look for the answers?" Julian asked, his straight nose chiselled white with sudden emotion. "It could have been a number of people close to us. It could even have been a member of the family, grown hard on avarice and bitter resentment. I was a very high-profile candidate as Sir Hugo's son. There has always been tension between the two families, I don't have to tell you that. But there was something truly terrible about it all. Something beyond the urge to make trouble, spread rumours. Something that was very personal and terribly malign. As far as I was concerned, Alyssa and Christopher were very much in love. Sometimes a woman's beauty can be a curse," Julian said. "I do know poor old Pat was very jealous of her."

"Then why not Patricia?" Brendon asked.

Julian shook his head. "I did consider Patricia, but in the end decided she didn't have enough hate in her. Besides, Pat can be a very silly woman. She would have given herself away. I've no doubt of that."

"My mother hated Alyssa, didn't she?" Brendon decided to bite the bullet.

"You're surely not suggesting your mother?" Julian asked, his voice a bit too loud.

"You don't have a good marriage, do you, Dad?" Brendon countered, facing an unpleasant truth. "You stay together, but you're not happy and it's getting worse, isn't it?"

The moment stretched out and out between them. Julian shifted his position in his leather chair. "I'm right, aren't I?" Brendon persisted. "Even at Charlotte's birthday party, Mum was so aloof, almost rude. I'm certain she didn't once smile. It's as though she hates Charlotte, as well."

There was a faint glaze in Julian Macmillan's fine grey eyes. "Charlotte is trouble, Bren," he said, very sombrely. "My heart aches for her. She's had to endure so much tragedy and neglect from her appalling family. I can't feel good about her inheriting this fortune and all it entails. It puts her, in many ways, in an unenviable position, always in the spotlight, in potential danger, but there was no way Sir Reginald was going to make Conrad his heir. Conrad simply lacked the necessary characteristics that make for success. He wasn't his brother. The boy, Simon, didn't even rate in the Old Man's eyes. The Old Man used to call him, quite cruelly, 'the crybaby.' Charlotte, even as a schoolgirl, showed great promise. Her grandfather made the judgement she could handle power when the time came. I believe that to be the case. I believe you do too, only Charlotte is going to be put through hoops—heaps of tests that wouldn't be inflicted on a young man. There are going to be years of doubts and uncertainties ahead for her. It's a huge burden, an onerous burden."

"But we're going to be there for her, aren't we, Dad? We're going to help her every inch of the way. We're going to support her. She needs us."

"I know," Julian confirmed, quietly. "You've always been extremely protective of Charlie, haven't you, Bren?"

"Well, I don't think of her as my little sister," Brendon retorted, dryly. "The little sister I never had, by the way."

His father's long fingers drummed the top of his desk. "Your mother didn't want any more children. Yours was a difficult birth."

Brendon shook his head. "Not true, Dad. It wasn't a difficult birth. Granddad told me."

His father sighed. "He would, probably for the best. I must tell you, your mother was absolutely delighted with you. You were enough. You know you are the son I've always wanted. You're the apple of your grandfather's eye. Your upbringing was far different than Charlotte's. You've always been surrounded by people who love and admire you. By the way, there's already gossip about you and Charlotte floating around Chambers," Julian said, staring at his son while waiting for a reaction.

"Charlie is just a baby." Brendon shrugged the gossip off.

"*Your* baby," his father said pointedly.

"Okay, so how does it look to Mum?" Brendon asked. "Does talk of Charlotte and me bring out her dark side?"

Julian frowned heavily. "*What* dark side?"

"The one you know about, Dad." Brendon's retort was as sharp as a knife. "To be attracted to a beautiful married woman is no sin. It's what you do about it that matters. Taking into account the harm an affair could cause. We'll never live down that terrible car crash, entirely innocent or not. It was just so heartbreaking. It left Charlie, a twelve-year-old, on her own, except for her grandfather, who was immersed in his many business interests. I believe you when you say there was no affair. Charlotte believes you."

"Does she? I'm so glad."

"She's been having flashbacks recently. I know they scare her, and Charlie doesn't scare easily. For some reason she's frightened of her uncle."

Julian sat straight, looking momentarily shaken. "Conrad has never done his duty by his son or his niece, but we all think he is fairly harmless."

"I beg to disagree. He's not harmless, Dad. Conrad Mansfield is a born actor. He just keeps the harm buried deep. If it could be proved that Christopher and not Conrad wrote *Cries of the Heart*, what do you think he might do if Charlotte threatened to expose him?"

"Aaah!" Julian gave a deep groan. "He would be desperate to keep it secret. I don't think he could handle the public humiliation. The world at large thinks Conrad Mansfield wrote the book. Now that we're discussing it, I never judged him to be a man of such deep feeling. To us insiders, the book was largely about *our* families. Laura was Alyssa, to my mind."

Brendon took a deep breath. "Well, you knew her, Dad. So, why did everyone accept that Conrad had pulled off a masterpiece?"

Julian leaned forward. "Because not a one of us knew any different. We were all gutted by the tragedy. It was so recent, so *real.* Christopher was my friend, but he never confided in me or anyone else that he had written a book. Christopher, right up until his death, was kept extremely busy. Sir Reginald saw to that. Both brothers were artistic. Both had a love and a knowledge of literature and beautiful things. They were raised in wealth. That's another problem for Charlotte. She'll never get Conrad out of Clouds."

"Trust me, Dad, she will. He'll be out in the New Year," Brendon said. "Charlotte has made up her mind. She's also said she wouldn't expose her uncle until after his death. That's only if we're right, of course."

Julian Macmillan blew out a breath. "Might be a wise move, if a difficult decision. It would create hell for her. What I don't understand is, why didn't Charlotte ask to read what Conrad has already written?"

Brendon looked up to meet his father's eyes. "Charlotte has

heart. She pitied him. She wanted time to think. I really came to tell you about that fool Simon, but I got sidetracked."

"So, fire away."

"Simon tried a foolhardy stunt with us as we were coming down from the mountain last night."

"*What?*" Julian reacted strongly.

"He was behind us in his BMW, driving much too fast. He passed us, then a short distance off he hit his brakes. That caused me to stand on mine. It was as close as one could come to the site of the Mansfield tragedy. It shook Charlotte up, as it was meant to. She memorized the rego. I checked it. Simon Mansfield. He had his girlfriend in the car. Oddly enough, she's a nice girl, not what you'd expect at all."

"She would be largely chosen for her ability to fade into the background," Julian said with his intimate knowledge of the Mansfield family. "Sir Reginald, wicked old soul that he was, decided on Julia not only because she was the love of your grandfather's life, but because she was the opposite of feisty. Julia was very unhappily married to Sir Reginald, God rest his soul," he said with great irony.

"Why did Granddad let him do it?" Brendon asked, not a young man to let the love of his life go.

"Julia found Reginald very exciting." Julian sighed. "She prized his cleverness, his ambition, his undoubted charisma. She wasn't as wise as she imagined herself to be. It didn't take long for cold reality to set in. Though, I'm obligated to say, Julia wanted for nothing outside a close, loving relationship with her husband. She had money to burn. It cost a small fortune getting the garden at Clouds underway. She was given free rein. Chris was her favourite. She loved little Charlotte, and she loved Alyssa, who was so very sweet to her. After they were killed, she simply pined away. It can happen. It did happen. I don't even know if Sir Reginald noticed she was gone."

"That's a terrible thing to say, Dad."

"I don't care!" Julian picked up his coffee cup, drank the contents down. "It's true. Sir Reginald had more than a touch of cruelty in him. My father was supposed to be his best friend. They'd been through University together. They founded Mansfield-Macmillan together. Sir Reginald trusted my father all his life, but trust was gone for my father once he lost Julia. Of course, there were many rotten things Sir Reginald did throughout their careers, but it was always about losing Julia. Then she died, much too early. My father was a one-woman man. I can say it now that my mother has passed. Dad loved her and she loved him, but Julia was his *great* love. I guess we all have one."

"Who's yours, Dad? No point in saying Mum," Brendon spoke bluntly. Simon and his dangerous antics were temporarily put aside. These were other things he really wanted to know.

Julian met his son's searching eyes. "If I could have had one woman in all the world, the one I would have chosen would have been Alyssa," he confessed, "but Christopher had already won her hand. That was it! So I married your mother, an elegant and refined young woman. I was determined to make her happy. *I* was determined to be happy."

"Only it all went wrong when your wife plumbed how you really felt?"

Julian nodded fiercely. "You've never been under any illusions, Bren. I know that. I worked very hard to make your mother happy. You never saw any sign of discord between us when you were growing up. Both of us wanted you to have the best life possible, a happy, stable home. That's what you got."

"So Mum would have felt no warmth towards Alyssa from very early on?"

"It was hardly Alyssa's fault that I had *feelings* for her." Julian made a conscious effort to keep calm. "Those feelings were never spoken of, never hinted at, never aired."

"Except women are aware of such things," Brendon said. "They don't have to dig for answers, they just *know*."

"We men understand that, Bren," his father said. "It was an attraction that went *nowhere*. Alyssa loved Christopher. She had made her choice. I accepted that. I am not a predatory man. I am not a dishonourable man."

"Of course you're not, Dad. Only Mum *knew*, and someone else knew," Brendon said. "Someone who hated both you and Alyssa."

Julian's grey eyes, the eyes his son had inherited, darkened to slate. His emotions, normally kept under control, had been brought to an unexpected head by his son's questions. "The only leads I had led nowhere, and I deliberately provoked answers. The deaths of Alyssa and Christopher, as you can imagine, came like a stab in the heart. I freely admit I've never gotten over the tragedy. I bury myself in my work."

"Work isn't the answer, Dad," Brendon said. "I worry about you. I worry about Mother. If you divorced, both of you could have the chance at a better life. You're a distinguished man, and you look great! If Mum would only loosen up a bit, she would have no difficulty finding a partner who could love her."

"You're missing something extremely telling, Bren," Julian said, his chiselled features grown taut. "Your mother loves *me*."

"I know it. I see it," Brendon said emphatically. "Are you saying you can never leave her?"

Julian put his glasses back on his nose. "That's exactly what I'm saying, Bren."

"You mean, you have no choice in the matter?" Brendon asked, thinking all chance of future happiness for the father he loved was cast to the wind.

"Brendon, your mother has demonstrated her devotion to me all these years. I'm not going to let her down. It would kill her, I promise."

Brendon shook his dark, handsome head, almost despairingly. "Mum is lucky to have *you*, Dad. You've set yourself a hard course. We have friends in our circle who are divorcing. Most of them have gone on to find other partners. I love my mother, but I do know she doesn't offer much in the way of lightheartedness."

"That's her nature, son." Julian sighed. "Not every woman can be so vibrant they capture attention. Take young Charlotte. She has the Mansfield colouring, the blond hair and the green eyes. She doesn't have the Mansfield height. Alyssa was petite. Charlotte is starting to look more and more like her mother, even to the cleft in her chin. Alyssa had that. Charlotte is as much her mother's daughter as her father's. There's no question Conrad and Patricia did everything in their power to make Alyssa feel unwelcome. She could have complained about them to Sir Reginald, but she never did."

"Maybe she should have," Brendon considered. "So, the more Charlotte gets to resemble her mother, the more *my* mother is going to dislike her?" he asked crisply and half-shook his head.

"I don't like it any more than you do," Julian acknowledged his deep disappointment.

Brendon gazed back at his father, allowing his anger to show. "Hang on, have the two of you spoken about it?"

"Brendon, I'm sorry." Julian raised his hand. "I've said my piece many times, but for all my efforts, your mother doesn't like the way you look at Charlotte. She doesn't like the way you've always looked out for her, from boyhood. She would much prefer you to turn your attention to another young woman we know. God knows there are enough of them out there interested in you."

Brendon sat back, understanding that nothing was simple in life. Certainly not his life. Women could and did go crazy with jealousy. "So, one reason Charlotte was hardly ever invited into our home was because my mother didn't want her around?" he asked, openly angry.

Julian's sigh was deep. "Brendon, I can't see it changing. Your mother has a very intense nature."

Brendon knew that well. "All these years later, and Mum hasn't outrun her jealousy," he said. "You've dug a deep pit for yourself, Dad."

Julian Mansfield threw up his hands in defeat. "Hardly anyone gets to live a life free of regret, Brendon," he said intensely. "I stay with your mother because I believe that if I left her, she would stray perilously close to taking her own life. She's that kind of woman."

Brendon felt so much like choking, he had to unfasten his collar and yank down his silk tie. "God, Dad! How long have you believed this?"

"For too long," Julian said quietly. "I believe it so strongly I've been forced to yield."

"It's emotional blackmail, and you could be wrong." Brendon was getting a highly unwelcome image of his mother.

"I'm not wrong, Bren. I'm answering your questions as truthfully as I can. Questions you're entitled to ask."

There was an implacable light in Brendon's eyes. "I'll never stop looking out for Charlotte, Dad."

"That could be because you not only love her, you're *in* love with her, son," Julian said quietly.

Brendon shook his head. "Charlotte doesn't want to get mixed up with us. She knows how to avoid the dangers. She sure as hell wouldn't tolerate Mum's coldness. But Charlotte and I are friends, comrades. I won't be offering her any ring, if that's what everyone seems to think. She wouldn't take it anyway. She'd be better off picking a name out of a hat."

* * *

Brendon had no sooner returned to his office, his face reflecting his anger and upset, when Charlotte walked through the open door. Her green eyes swept over him. "What is it, Bren? What's happened?" Her voice was urgent. She had caught the bleakness in him.

Brendon managed to lighten his expression. "Shut the door, Charlie."

"Sure." Charlotte did so.

"You needn't worry. I'm just a bit browned off," he said briskly. "I've a question of my own." He waved her into a chair. "What are we going to do about your cousin? He's certain to deny the incident happened. He'll have his puppet-on-a-string girlfriend to back him up."

Charlotte lowered her tote bag to the carpet. "I've already taken that into account, but I have a feeling Carol *won't* lie for him. Carol doesn't strike me as a liar."

"Intuition again?" Brendon's head was crammed with visions of Charlotte right through their entwined lives: her cleverness, her spirit, her animation. He knew now what his father had been talking about when he spoke of Alyssa.

"Certainly, but I know people who know Carol," Charlotte said. "She's had her head turned by Simon. He *is* handsome. He's rich. I daresay, if you agreed with him all the time, he could be pleasant enough. Carol hasn't had enough time to judge his character."

"He doesn't have any character." Brendon's tone was scornful. "He's the classic example of a guy who has gotten by on the family connections. He has never had the slightest interest in emulating his uncle Christopher or his grandfather."

"It's beyond him, Bren. He can't help that. Having a brilliant grandfather is no guarantee the rest of us would inherit his formidable business brain."

Brendon lowered his head into his hands. "I'm not saying that, but Simon's had enough training in business to hold down a decent job. Currently he doesn't have a job. He's a firm believer in the pleasure principle. He's living such a luxurious lifestyle even *his* inheritance can run out. What then? Is he going to come begging to you at some point in the future?"

Charlotte found she couldn't relax, not with Brendon looking so stressed. "Didn't one of the Vanderbilts say that inherited wealth is certain death to ambition?"

Brendon felt his tension ease. "If you say so." There was amusement back in his eyes. "What concerns me is Simon's bad relationship with you."

"Wealth does affect relationships, Bren," Charlotte pointed out. "All sorts of relationships, even with you and me. The burden outweighs the advantages. As far as Grandpa's various companies go, he put highly competent men in charge. I'm leaving them in place. At this point there's no need for change in any of the outfits. I'm certain these men will work well for me, but I'll be calling regular meetings. I want to learn. I intend to ask for their help and support. Business has always been male-oriented, but more and more women are crashing through the glass ceiling."

"They are, I'm happy to say, but what about your law career?" Brendon asked. Charlotte would make a brilliant barrister, even a QC one day.

"It *was* to be my future, Bren, but my whole life has changed. You know that. It'll be more than enough for me learning the ropes. Grandfather's enterprises can't stand still. They have to go from strength to strength. There must be scope for expansion, new enterprises, medical science, technology, renewable energy. Take your pick. It's a new age. I care about my country. I care about doing good with all this money, far more than I could possibly need in a long, lavish lifetime. I have had the odd moment when I've thought of giving most of the money away and living my own life, out of the limelight, using my own talents."

"But you feel the responsibility?" He knew that was the case.

"I do."

Brendon nodded. He found himself comparing Charlotte's strength with that of her uncle and cousin. Sir Reginald had made a hard choice, but a good choice. He had every confidence in Charlotte. As a rule, the professional men he knew saw themselves as superior to their female counterparts. With successful women he had found a broader sense of purpose. Charlotte sat before him dressed in a short, form-fitting black dress that showed off her pale gold legs of summer, paired with a short white linen jacket. Her glazed black tote bag sat at her feet. She was wearing her familiar high-heeled pumps in black patent leather. Her beautiful hair was drawn back from her face. Diamond studs flashed in her ears. She looked stunning. That was the norm for Charlotte.

"You Macmillans are big shareholders in Grandfather's companies," she was saying. "Your grandfather and your father sit on most of the boards."

"They do, but many was the time your grandfather overrode company decisions. Sir Reginald was a ruthless operator," Brendon said. "He didn't give a damn about victims of his manipulations. There are stories galore about that."

"So I believe," Charlotte said coolly, "but things will change. Ruthless or not, Grandpa gave away millions. To most people the amount is staggering. Let's not forget that."

"No one is forgetting it," Brendon responded just as coolly. "Though there was always method in it," he added dryly.

She met his beautiful light eyes, aware of the powerful complex intimacy between them. "I want you to sit on some of the boards, Bren." She sat watching him, waiting.

"Oh, Charlie, baby!" he groaned.

"I *need* you, Bren," she said with great conviction. "And I'm determined to get you. We're of like mind. I trust you."

"Are you saying you don't trust my grandfather and father?" He grimaced.

For a while Charlotte said nothing. "I trust you more," she said finally. "You know where I want to go."

"What if I do?" He shrugged. "You'd need a lot more support to get me voted onto any board. Even colleagues in Chambers aren't all that happy with my rise to power."

"That's what power is all about, Bren," Charlotte said, "getting things done. If I want you, no one is going to stand in my way. I believe we need to invest more in industry, in innovation. We're the future, Bren. We need to be whiz kids. We need to take whiz kids on board. Surround ourselves with them. Give them the necessary backing to achieve their goals."

"You're very ambitious, Charlotte," he said, understanding her aims perfectly.

"Aren't you as well? We're ambitious for ourselves to a degree, but we're ambitious for our country. Isn't that right?"

"Dead-right," Brendon said. "But first we have to solve the problem of Simon, and after that, your uncle Conrad. We can't leave things as they are."

"I know that," Charlotte said irritably. "Carol works in the university library. I'm thinking of calling in on her."

"What, today?" One of Brendon's dark brows shot up.

"What better day? I'll sound her out. Despite her being heavily under Simon's influence, I think she'll go with the truth. If Simon wasn't trying to run us off the road, he was definitely trying to scare us."

Brendon remembered those long moments of anger and anxiety. "He took one hell of a risk with our lives, and his for that matter. I suppose you can find out what Carol has to say. I'm not at all convinced she'll go against him. I'd come with you, only I have to finish this for Dad." He slapped a hand down hard on a pile of files.

Charlotte stood up, gathering her tote bag. "That's okay. I'll ring you later to tell you what she told me. We have to take time out pretty soon to discuss future plans, Bren. You probably know, the word around town is that we're an item."

Brendon rose from behind his desk, intending to walk her to the elevator. "We've always been an item, Charlie," he said crisply, choosing to ignore her teasing.

"We have been, haven't we, though that might require reassessment." She flashed him a smile that was pure mischief.

Brendon let his eyes linger on her, but what he felt, what he wanted to do, he had to shut off. He hadn't been given free rein. There were complications that ruled their relationship. He couldn't imagine Charlotte tolerating his mother's barely veiled hostility. His deeply reserved mother could control her tongue, but she couldn't control the expression in her dark eyes. He could scarcely believe his mother could set herself against Charlotte, hardly more than a girl, but she had. The problem was real. His mother blamed Charlotte for the sins of Alyssa. Innocent or not. He realized now his mind had registered that even as a child. As soon as he got back to his office, he would tip off Charlotte's minders that she was heading for the university library. He had a bad feeling about Simon Mansfield.

Charlotte had no difficulty finding Carol. In fact, Carol looked so pleased to see her she greeted Charlotte with a kiss on the cheek.

"I won't take you from your work," Charlotte whispered, her eyes sweeping the library she knew so well from her student days.

"Over here," Carol said, leading the way to a quiet section of the library. "It's about the other night, isn't it?" she asked, sounding immensely apologetic.

Charlotte nodded. "What Simon did was incredibly dangerous, Carol, you do realize that?"

Carol's face fell. "Of course I do. I couldn't believe he could be so reckless."

"Simon chose to intercept us at almost the exact spot where my parents' car went over the side of the mountain into the valley below," Charlotte told her.

Carol's smooth skin blanched. "Oh, Charlotte, I'm so sorry. Simon couldn't have realized that, could he?"

"All of us know the exact spot, Carol. My father was Simon's uncle."

"You're saying he *meant* to be so cruel?" Carol asked, aghast.

"That's exactly what I'm saying. Simon has been brought up to believe he's a law unto himself. He also believes he's better than anyone else. I know you have feelings for him, but I also believe you don't know him. You haven't had the time. I bet he's already asked you to cover for him about the incident?"

Carol smoothed back one side of her pageboy. "He does expect me to back whatever story he tells," she confessed. "He's ready to deny the whole episode. My *duty,* apparently, is to corroborate his story if worse comes to worst."

"So, what are you going to do?" Charlotte struggled to keep her voice low.

Carol's response was immediate. "Don't worry, Charlotte. I'm not going to lie."

Charlotte held back a sigh of relief. She took the other young woman's hand. "I knew you wouldn't, Carol. You stick to your principles."

"Well, I try to." Carol attempted a smile.

"There are a few things you have to do," Charlotte warned her. "Don't have Simon come around to your apartment. Don't be alone with him. Simon has a vile temper. You need to protect yourself. He won't take your perceived desertion lightly."

"Don't I know it." Carol felt a flash of fear, remembering how Simon had so cruelly squeezed her hand. "But he would never really hurt me, surely?" she asked with a quick intake of breath.

"He'd be a fool to try it. You have friends, Carol. Just remember that Simon is very unpredictable. Let him know you refuse to lie about what happened. I repeat, don't be alone with him. If Simon attempts to harass you, we can arrange for a AVO, an apprehended violence order, to be taken out."

"Oh, no, no, no!" Carol's cry attracted attention. A group of students had even stopped work to listen. Carol lowered her voice to a near whisper. "There's no need for that, Charlotte. Simon is not an abusive man. I mean, he's a Mansfield. He's Sir Reginald Mansfield's grandson. He wouldn't bring shame on himself or the family."

"All he needs is for you to keep quiet, Carol. He expects you to keep quiet. If you stayed with him, he would always expect it. Your function would be to back him at all times."

Carol felt sick. "I have to accept that you know Simon far better than I do, Charlotte. I won't lie for him. Not now, not ever. I couldn't live with myself. I'll do what you say."

"The slightest sign of trouble, give me a call," Charlotte said, handing Carol a card she had taken from her bag. "Any one of those numbers. I have minders keeping an eye out for me. They think I don't know they're there, but I do. You'll get help if you need it, but I hope I'm proved wrong." Even as she said it, Charlotte knew Simon would most certainly lie in wait for his *ex*-girlfriend.

Out on the street, Charlotte caught sight of her two burly minders pretending to be in deep conversation. She smiled to herself. They had blown their cover and still didn't know it. In one way their day-in, day-out presence annoyed her. On the other hand, she realized most probably she was in need of it. Of course, Brendon knew all about the arrangement. The Macmillans had judged she needed it. She was in the most danger from her own family.

Chapter 7

Simon expected he might have a bit of trouble gaining admission to Carol's apartment block. He needn't have worried. As he moved to the security door, two giggling young women, dressed in his view like a couple of tarts, were emerging. One good thing about Carol was that she didn't giggle. She didn't dress like a tart, either. Not that he cared much for the way she did dress. That would have to change.

"Off to a party, then?" He gave them his best smile. It always worked. "Happy Christmas, by the way."

"Happy Christmas to you, too." The young women had sighted the handsome, oh so toffee-nosed Simon a number of times before. They knew who he was. That only increased the giggles. They held the door for him, noting his stylish gear.

"Many thanks," he said suavely. "Enjoy yourselves."

"Oh, we will, handsome laddie!" The plump one affected a stage Irish accent, while the other shrieked with laughter. They waved to him cheekily, and then went happily on their way.

No doubt they were wondering how Carol got to be so lucky landing him, a fabulous catch. Not even Carol understood.

He was in. It had been all too easy. He expected life to go his way. He confidently expected Carol to welcome him. He hadn't rung. There was no need. She was the one who had rung him, bleating like a silly sheep about how she couldn't break the rules for him. It was a bit of a problem, but she would come 'round after he made it clear it was in her own interests to do so. Unlike his cousin, Carol didn't have powerful people protecting her. Carol only had elderly parents—respectable people, of course, but of no account.

On the eighth floor, Carol had settled in to watching one of her favourite TV series.

When she realized someone was knocking on the door, she pressed Mute on the remote. She wasn't expecting anyone. Simon would have had to buzz her apartment for her to open the security door. It wasn't Simon. Of course not. The phone rang, further startling her. She went to it, spoke a little nervously into the receiver. "Hello?"

"It's Charlotte, Carol," came a charming, low-pitched female voice. "I'm just checking to see that you're okay."

The knocking continued, diverting Carol's attention. "I'm fine, thank you, Charlotte," Carol replied, feeling a warm glow that someone like Charlotte Mansfield cared. "Really, I am."

"That's good."

"Thank you so much for ringing. I appreciate it."

"Is that knocking?" Charlotte asked.

"Someone is at the door," Carol said.

"Did you buzz them in?" Charlotte was instantly on the alert. Carol Sutton was a young woman way out of her depth.

"It'll be my neighbour. People are dropping off cards and little Christmas presents," Carol explained. "I'd better go, Charlotte."

"Be careful now," Charlotte said.

"I will," Carol promised. She hung up, and then moved quickly to the door, a smile on her face. It was most likely Mrs. Davis in number four. If it was, they could watch TV together. She knew Mrs. Davis enjoyed the series she was watching as much as she did.

Charlotte, who had dropped in at a friend's pre-Christmas party, intending to stay only a short time, went in search of Brendon, who, like her, was invited everywhere as a matter of course. She couldn't find him. There was such a crush. She left a message for him with her hostess, saying she was popping in on their friend, Carol, for a half hour. She was *keen* to see her. She stressed the *keen*. Carol was home. Alone. Carol in many ways was a fragile person. Charlotte's warning antennae was working overtime.

For an instant Carol went into free fall when she discovered it was Simon at her door. In the next instant, she relaxed as soon as she saw that the smile on his lips matched the smile in his eyes. "I would have buzzed, but two girls were going out, on their way to a party," he explained, sounding happy for once. "I wanted to see you. I hate it when we fall out, especially when we so rarely do."

Once inside the door, Simon pulled the unresisting Carol to him, dipping his head to kiss her full on the mouth. "Wouldn't have a whiskey on hand, would you?" In high spirits, he all but bounced into the up-market apartment Carol's parents had bought her when she moved out of home. It was modestly furnished. Modest. Just like Carol.

Carol, a very sparing drinker, mostly white wine, had bought an expensive bottle of single-malt Scotch for him, a twelve-year-old Glenfiddich, knowing how much he liked it.

"Join me, won't you?" Simon called as Carol went off to find the unopened bottle.

"I won't, Simon. I don't like the taste of whiskey."

"Actually, I approve of your being a non-drinker, or near enough. I don't like women drinking. They have no head for it."

"Some definitely do," said Carol, thinking of several women of her acquaintance who could drink Simon under the table. "Just a drop of water?" she asked, knowing she had to get things right. "I do have ice."

"A couple of ice cubes, whiskey over, no water," Simon instructed. "I'm so sorry about the other night. I don't know what got into me. I deeply regret I shocked you."

"You did shock me, Simon," Carol said very seriously. She found a crystal tumbler, dropped two cubes of ice into it, and then poured the Scotch, measuring off the correct amount. "If the incident comes to anything, it's as I told you, Simon. I can't—I won't—lie."

What a crying shame! "I expect Charlotte or Macmillan has contacted you?" he asked as she came toward him, offering him his drink. "Turn the TV off, won't you? I don't know why you like that show. It's so dreary."

"It's true to the times, terrible times, Simon. Britain at war. All the bombings, the destruction, the deaths, privations, lack of just about everything, including food. We don't know how lucky we are."

"Spare me the lecture, dear one," he drawled. "Sit down. Here, beside me." He patted the sofa, which barely passed muster, in his opinion. "When are you going to start doing up the apartment? I can help you. Not that it really matters if we're going to get married." He put his arm around her shoulders, kissed her neck.

Carol tried to stay unaffected. Simon was the only man to kiss her on the neck. "I did speak to Charlotte," she said, watching him down his Scotch in two gulps. Surely as a whiskey connoisseur, he should be savouring it? "I promised her I'd tell the truth about the incident. She said you staged it almost at the spot where her parents crashed over the cliff."

"And you believed her?" Simon set the crystal tumbler down much too hard. His tone had completely changed.

Carol nodded bravely. "I did. Can't you see that it's madness, Simon, your bitter resentment of your cousin? We have to be accountable for our actions. What you did up there on the mountain was *criminal*."

"Criminal? Well, you are ablaze with bravado, aren't you? I'd advise you to leave it," Simon said very tightly indeed. He caught her hand and squeezed it hard, the punishment of choice.

"I'm not sure I can. Please let go of my hand, Simon. You're hurting me."

Simon laughed out loud. "You amaze me. How can I be hurting you by holding your hand?"

"You're not holding it, you're squeezing it," Carol said, tremors running up her legs.

Simon appeared not to hear her. "I never *meant* to do it, you know. Something got into me."

Carol wrenched her hand away. Whiteness surrounded her wrist like a bracelet. She resisted the urge to rub it. "You must change, Simon," she said. "I do care about you, but I can't lie for you, and neither can I possibly marry you."

Simon threw back his blond head. "I haven't asked you yet. Beside the girls I used to date, you look like the hired help."

Dignity shone out of Carol's eyes. "I'm quite sure you're the only person who has ever thought it."

"Are you kidding? Everyone is wondering what I see in you," he said cruelly.

"Well, people are wondering what I see in *you*, as well," Carol retorted. "You can save yourself right now, Simon." She spoke with as much firmness as she could muster, though her heart was hammering so hard she thought she might faint. "I'd like you to leave. I was a fool to let you in."

Simon flushed a dull red. He was shaken, though he would never admit it. He had thought he had control of Carol. If she was now showing spirit, he had his cousin, Charlotte, to blame. "You could have been something more, Carol. Now you're back to nothing. You're a—" He broke off angrily as the buzzer on the intercom sounded.

"You're expecting someone else?" he demanded.

Carol took her chance. She jumped up. "It's probably my friend Beth. She said she might pop over."

"That silly bitch! Like I'm in the mood for this. Tell her to go away. Tell her I'm here. That should shift her."

The security video showed Charlotte, standing outside. Carol didn't speak. Instead she opened the security door, allowing Charlotte in. Something else was working her way, she realized. She hadn't shut the front door properly after Simon. It was very slightly ajar. Charlotte would be able to get in.

"I don't think you realize what it means going against me, Carol," Simon was saying. "You'll have no future whatever. I have connections all over. If I exert a little pressure, you could even lose your cushy job at the library."

Carol shook her head. "I'd say *not.* You'd have no influence whatever at the library."

Simon was severely taken aback. "We'll see about that!" he huffed with his customary self-confidence.

"I'm not bothered, Simon. I'm very good at what I do, but I have no future with you. That is now clear. Sooner or later we show ourselves in our true colours. You're a born bully. You messed with my head. I let you. I see now that you want a bit of power so you tried to exert it over me. It nearly worked. I don't believe you could make any girl happy. You've probably been rejected a few times, come to that!"

"You think so?" Simon stared back at Carol as if he didn't even know who she was. He stood up, a tall young man over six feet, coming to tower over Carol, who was wearing comfortable flatties.

Carol didn't back away. Instead she gave him a look almost of pity. "I want you to go, Simon." She felt empowered by the knowledge that Charlotte was on her way up. "I so expected more of you."

"Did you now?" Simon was in one of the worst rages of his life. "Did you expect this?" He struck out at this new, defiant Carol, succumbing to his anger. "Consider this a little wake-up call," he snarled.

The force of his hard, openhanded slap sent Carol reeling. It was a truly terrible moment. Carol made a clutch at an armchair, her ears ringing. Simon Mansfield was beyond the pale. She had been warned. She had ignored the warnings. She had brought it all on herself.

Charlotte, when she entered the apartment, found them, frozen into some sort of tableau. Carol was cowering in an armchair, holding her hand to her burning, smarting cheek and eye, Simon was towering over her, emanating menace. He broke his pose at Charlotte's precipitous entrance, his blond head snapping around.

"What the hell are you doing here?" he shouted. "Get the hell out!"

His fury left Charlotte untouched. "Are you all right, Carol?" she asked swiftly, feeling somehow responsible for her appalling cousin.

Carol couldn't speak she was so distressed, but she flashed Charlotte a look of tangible relief.

"What a bullying bastard you are, Simon." Charlotte turned back to him, her expression one of disgust. "You think hitting Carol will make your problems disappear?"

"She'll get over it." Simon badly wanted to hit his cousin, as well. She deserved it. This was the cousin who had ruined his life.

"You've got no idea have you, you poser? Carol wants you out of her life. She despises you. So do I. To think that you've turned into one of those vile men who abuses women."

Simon felt his fist clench and unclench. "Yeah, I've heard all about you and your views on domestic abuse, the sizeable sums of money you hand out to shelters. Ever think these women bring it on themselves? There's two sides to a story, you know."

"Problems will never be solved by violence, you brute." Even in her high heels, no way could Charlotte measure up to him, yet she looked completely in control of the situation. "Want to hit me too, do you, Simon?" she challenged, her green eyes as brilliant as precious stones.

"I'm trying to decide." His jaw was so tight the words barely escaped him. He hadn't completely lost it. He couldn't lay a hand on Charlotte. Not a finger.

"It's a huge leap from striking Carol to striking *me*," his cousin said, standing her ground.

A kind of dread was flooding Simon's chest. Charlotte was who she was. The Mansfield heiress. Macmillan would kill him if he dared to touch her. Panic prickled through him. He wouldn't have thought it possible that poor old Carol would betray him. He was seeing now he'd made a huge mistake. The urge to hit out at his cousin was so strong he had to lace his fingers tightly together.

The apartment door was thrown back so hard it hit the wall. A moment more and Brendon Macmillan appeared, looking utterly dangerous. He was never far from Charlotte, Simon thought, trying desperately to compose himself.

"What's going on here?" Brendon's voice was so sharp it sliced the air. His heart contracted as he went to Charlotte first, putting his hand on her shoulder. "You okay? I got your message." Always, always, the powerful urge to protect her.

"Thank God for that." For a split second she rested her head against his shoulder.

Over on the sofa, Carol, head in hands, was quietly sobbing.

"What's this got to do with you, Macmillan?" Simon cried, hot-faced and furious, unable to accept humiliation. All his so-called power and influence meant nothing, he realized. He had no power at all. Not like that bastard Macmillan.

Carol looked up. "Hello, Brendon," she said piteously. Her eyes were mere slits from the crying, stinging, and swelling of her face.

Brendon took in her sad state, wanting to give Charlotte's cousin the thrashing he deserved. Carol's left cheek was a dull red. The swelling was around her eye. She would have a black eye by morning. "I'm so very, very sorry about this, Carol," Brendon said, releasing a hard breath. He looked at Charlotte. "You might want to ring the police, Charlie. Report a domestic disturbance."

"Oh . . . oh . . . please don't!" Carol cried out a desperate entreaty. She rose shakily to her feet. "I don't want any police here, Brendon. My parents would be terribly shocked. It's nearly Christmas."

"Besides, there's no crime." Unbelievably, Simon dismissed Carol's sad state. "I threw out my hand and inadvertently caught Carol's cheek."

Brendon turned on him with a tightening of his muscles. He was totally disgusted with Simon Mansfield. He got a grip on the lapels of Simon's expensive jacket and then slammed him so hard up against the wall, the adjacent framed print fell down. "Were you going to hit Charlotte, too?" he asked grimly, looking like a man just waiting for the chance to lash out.

Simon found himself covered in sweat. "Of course not," he spluttered. "I didn't touch you, did I, Charlotte?"

Brendon didn't remove his hands, or slacken his hold. "You need to back off, Mansfield. Back right off."

"Okay, okay!" Simon knew he couldn't possibly pick a fight with Brendon Macmillan. His strength was far superior. As it was, Macmillan was just about lifting him off his feet.

"Apologize to Carol," Brendon urged. "Tell her you will never bother her again. *Mean* it."

Simon swallowed hard. "I'm sorry, Carol," he muttered, his insides burning with humiliation. "It was an accident. I wouldn't hurt you for the world. I'll clear out now. I won't be coming back."

Carol, who had crumpled under the cowardly attack, abruptly took charge. She was sickened and trembling. "See that you don't, or I'll take action against you, Simon. It will make the papers."

"Think of the exposure, Simon," Macmillan said in a mocking tone. "A strike against you. Some people will be delighted with that. You're not exactly popular around town." He released Simon abruptly, watching him slump at his feet.

"You've been warned, Simon. Let this be an end to it." Charlotte spoke quietly, but the message rang out, loud and clear.

"I'll see you to the door, shall I?" Brendon gave Simon a shove in the back.

Simon went quietly. Hatred was swelling in his chest and running down his arms. Hitting a woman had come as much as a shock to him as it had to Carol. His behaviour was getting out of control. He knew what he had to do. He had to keep his head down.

Charlotte spotted the bottle of Glenfiddich on the counter. In the galley kitchen, she found a glass, pouring a small measure of the whiskey into it and topping it up with a little water.

"I think you can do with a drop of this, Carol. No need to sip it. Get it down. It won't hurt you. We'll stay with you until you feel better."

Carol took a large swallow of the whiskey, coughed a little, and felt the liquid run like fire into her stomach. "I bought it for Simon, you know," she said, halfway between laughing and crying.

"He won't be bothering you again, Carol," Brendon said. "Where are you spending Christmas?"

"With my parents," Carol said. "I always spend Christmas with my parents. Christmas is for family, isn't it?"

"Yes." Charlotte's answer was on the poignant side. She was thinking of the strangeness and the dysfunction of her own family, her parents taken so abruptly and violently away from her. She thought in that moment she had no one but Brendon, Brendon Macmillan, her defender. With no one else could she feel such a sense of *oneness*.

Brendon paid a visit to his parents' grand harbour side house the following balmy evening. He hadn't seen or spoken to his mother for almost a week. His father's cold case and his own affairs had kept him pretty well glued to his desk. He knew he would be expected for Christmas dinner, but he saw now he had to be with Charlotte, even if it meant hurting his mother.

The Christmas tree in the entrance hall looked wonderfully festive, decked out in multicoloured baubles. Brightly wrapped presents were piled at the tree's base. His mother hurried down the steps to greet him. She was wearing a blue dress, her favourite colour. She looked beautiful with a radiant smile on her face. The smile made *such* a difference.

"Darling, how lovely to see you!" she cried, her slender arms outstretched.

Brendon moved forward, producing his own smile. He bent his head to kiss his mother on both cheeks. As always, she was wearing a sweet, light perfume. "Lovely to see you, Mother." His mother had always preferred "Mother" to "Mum," though he often slipped up. This wasn't one of those days. His mother had a real gift for formality. "I thought I should call in. Dad has been keeping me busy."

"He's so proud of you, Brendon," his mother said. Her indulgent smile wrapped him in high favour. "We both are. I don't have to tell you how Sir Hugo dotes on you. We'll be having a few extras on Christmas Day. A couple of overseas guests. Not that I mind. I meant to tell you that you're very welcome to bring a special girlfriend along, if she's not spending the day with family. I know Lisa's family is still in London."

For a minute Brendon was at a loss for words. "They're not due back until the end of January," he said, finally. "Lisa is a special *friend*, Mother, but she's not my girlfriend. Not anymore. Lisa and I wouldn't work."

"But, darling, I thought she was everything you wanted?" His mother stroked his arm.

"You're going to have to stop trying to marry me off." Brendon tried to turn it into a joke.

"Brendon. Darling, I want to be able to hold my first grandchild in my arms. I want to kiss its sweet little face. A boy first, I hope, and then a daughter. Come into the living room. Would you like a cold drink? I won't offer alcohol, as you're driving. We Macmillans have to be doubly careful not to besmirch our reputation."

"I'm fine, thank you." Brendon took the bit between his teeth. He said without preamble, "I know you'll be disappointed, but I need to tell you that I have other plans for Christmas dinner."

His mother swung back, staring at him as though his decision was about as hurtful as one could get. Indeed, her expression was so angry at the idea of his defection, for an instant Brendon didn't know who this lissome, dark-haired, dark-eyed woman could be. "What are you saying?" she asked, implying he was being dreadfully disloyal and disrespectful.

Brendon had to marvel at how he had cut his mother's apron strings so early. He waited until his mother was seated, straight-backed, no slumping. "I think you know how fond I am of Charlotte," he said, taking an armchair on the opposite side of the large, circular French-lacquer cocktail table. On it sat a large crystal vase filled with beautiful, scented red roses, a few art books, and a pair of Meissen crested cockatoos, enamelled in pinks and yellows perched on blue and green tree stumps. They had been a gift to his mother from his father a few years back.

"Oh, Charlotte!" Olivia Macmillan's entire face had tightened. She threw up a dismissive hand. "You surely aren't going to tell me you want to spend Christmas Day with *her*?"

"I do. Charlotte is on her own. She has an appalling family who has never shown the slightest interest in her. In many ways, she's the poor little rich girl."

"I believe she has scores of friends," Olivia scoffed. "Can't she join any one of them for Christmas dinner? Better yet, I've heard on the grapevine that she is providing Christmas dinner for a number of her little charities. She could surely join them?"

Brendon realized he had to come to the point. "Why do you hate Charlotte?" he asked. "You've always hated her, even when she was a little girl."

"*Hate* her! What nonsense. I rarely think of her," Olivia imparted.

"Not true. I've always sensed, even as a boy, you disliked Charlotte. You never tried to take her under your wing, a simple kindness. That was as unfathomable to me then as now."

Olivia coloured a little. "Been talking to your father, have you?"

"Is there some reason why I shouldn't?" Brendon countered. "Dad and I are close. We talk, or at least we try to, every single day."

"You must tell me sometime what about," Olivia said with some sarcasm. "Your Charlotte is her *daughter*." A dark shadow fell over her face as she said it.

Now they were getting to the crux of the matter, Brendon thought. "When she was younger, she was all Mansfield," he pointed out.

"The colouring was only camouflage. She's Alyssa," Olivia muttered through clenched teeth.

"She's *not* Alyssa," Brendon said quietly, but firmly. "She's Charlotte, her own person. She's beautiful. She's outstandingly clever. She's compassionate and caring, a little bit of a firebrand, I admit. To my mind she's a truly exceptional woman."

"I would shove Charlotte Mansfield completely out of your mind, Brendon," his mother advised, her eyes fixed on him. "She's trouble."

"You can say that when you don't even know her?" Brendon asked, keeping to a level tone.

"I know she has the same kind of power as her mother. She turns men's heads," Olivia spoke in near despair.

"Isn't that likely to happen with beautiful women? I'm sure you've turned heads yourself, Mother."

Olivia inclined her glossy dark head. Not strictly beautiful, Olivia Macmillan was a striking-looking woman, if on the severe side.

"Only *I* know how to control myself. I know how to behave, how to live an honourable life. You can say I'm a role model for my generation. I didn't sleep around. I didn't steal other women's men."

"And you are saying Alyssa did?"

"That was the general opinion," Olivia said with a little moue of disgust.

"Your opinion, Mother. Only there's no truth behind it."

"I can't speak of her infidelity!" Olivia exploded. "I've pledged to forget it. Forgive."

Brendon's answer was quiet, even compassionate. "It's all very well to say that, Mother, but you're not by nature a forgiving person. In any case, there is nothing to forgive. Despite the years Dad has denied the charge, you can't leave it alone. You can't exorcise Alyssa from your mind. You can't even begin to acknowledge you might have been wrong."

"Well, men always stick together, don't they?" Olivia exclaimed bitterly. "After what you've had to say, Brendon, I'd like you to go."

"Certainly, Mother." Brendon stood up. "I'm sorry to disappoint you, but you'll have a house full of people. Charlotte has no one."

Olivia gave a cry of near-anguish. "She wants to take you from me. I think I've always known she would. Just like Alyssa took Julian. Julian showed how much he loved me by betraying me. You are set to do the same. That girl could have any number of men. I've seen the way they look at her. The way you look at her. She wants *you*, my son. She doesn't care a jot about me. It's all happened before."

Brendon felt his mother's pain, however abnormal, but he also felt compelled to say, "I think you should talk to a professional about this, Mum. You've allowed your jealousy of Alyssa to turn into an obsession. Charlotte doesn't even know my plans for Christmas Day. She'll be expecting me to be here with you and Dad and Granddad."

"Don't you understand anything at all?" Olivia cried, her dark eyes deepening to almost black. "She wants *you* to spite me."

Brendon felt a great upsurge of pity. "It's all in your head, Mum. I hate to see you so terribly upset. I feel sorry for you. I see now you could have been the one to set off all the rumours about Alyssa and Dad. Jealousy is a form of madness." An idea erupted out of nowhere. "It *was* you, wasn't it?" he asked.

"What on earth do you mean?"

Brendon met his mother's burning gaze head-on. "I think Dad has long suspected the truth, but never confronted you knowing what pressure that would put you under."

Olivia's face showed inner turmoil. Her voice sank to a whisper. "What if I did?" she admitted. "It was my only defence. I adored Julian. He was my whole life. I thought he loved me like I loved him, only one evening I saw him and Alyssa talking quietly out on the terrace together. They were facing one another. I couldn't make out what they were saying, but I could make out the look on my husband's face. I wasn't misled. Julian has never looked at me like that, not before or since. That woman stole my happiness. Mark my words, her daughter will betray you."

Brendon was totally unconvinced. "You don't know Charlotte at all. You don't know anything about her. It's easier to blame Dad than blame yourself." On edge, he continued, "Charlotte's parents are dead. Their car veered off the mountain and crashed into the valley below. Maybe they *were* arguing; they were arguing earlier. Maybe it got out of hand. But what were they arguing about? You don't see the role you played in that, Mum? You don't see that your truths were no more than sick imaginings. The Mansfields died too young. Charlotte lost her parents. She was orphaned."

"The situation was not created by *me*," Olivia spoke fiercely in her own defence. "I was the injured party. I have never regretted what I did, Brendon. Of course they argued. Christopher was such a fool. He worshipped her."

Brendon gave a deep, heartfelt groan. "I can't bear to dwell on this, the worst of it. You're my mother. I love you, but my feelings for you will never be the same."

Olivia's answer came in a haggard tone. "I'm only trying to protect you, Brendon. It's my duty."

"Then I relieve you of it." Brendon broke off with a jerk of the head, as unnoticed by him and his mother, his father had entered the living room, tall, handsome, a most memorable-looking man with a tense expression on his face.

"Relieve your mother of what, Bren?" Julian asked. He knew from long experience that when his wife shifted into a certain gear, there was no changing it.

"Nothing that matters, Dad." Brendon didn't want to involve his father in his upset.

"I think it matters very much," Julian Macmillan said, his eyes moving to his wife, sitting rigid on the sofa. "What's going on, Olivia?" he asked, his expression grim.

Olivia's laugh had not an ounce of humour in it. "Brendon was telling me he won't be joining us for Christmas Day, my dear. He intends to spend it with Charlotte Mansfield, of all people."

"And?" Julian advanced into the room.

"What do you mean, *and*?" Olivia retorted, her face suddenly overlaid with uncertainty.

"Our son can surely spend Christmas Day with whomever he pleases," Julian said.

"Oh, Julian!" Olivia cried, pressing her hand against her breast. "If he loved us he would be with us."

"Poor Liv!" Julian said quietly, seeing his wife's pallor. "You demand absolute allegiance, don't you? We have the best son in the world."

"Who will be corrupted by that Mansfield girl," Olivia cried out, near hysterically, unusual behaviour for such a self-contained woman.

"That will do, Olivia." Julian Macmillan abruptly showed an iron hand. "You've wasted more than half your lifetime on your jealousy of Alyssa Mansfield, and now her daughter. You've poisoned our marriage. I won't have it. Not any longer. You won't put Brendon through hoops. You have to make changes."

"Please, Dad," Brendon intervened, acutely conscious of his mother's stricken face.

"You go, Bren," Julian said. It was an order. "I'll see you tomorrow. Your mother and I need to have a long talk. I've been wrong to delay it. All I've done is feed the flames. I absolutely refuse to countenance any attack on Charlotte. I owe that to her parents."

Olivia raised her head quickly. "You've never persuaded me, Julian," she accused. "You loved Alyssa Mansfield. There's no getting away from that."

"So you set out on your dangerous course," Julian said, "indifferent to possible consequences. I will say this for the last time. Every rumour you somehow managed to put out there was a lie, a mean-spirited desire to strike at a woman entirely innocent."

"A woman you can't bear to talk about." Olivia had the thrust of the last word.

Chapter 8

Brendon let himself out of the house with one of Karl Marx's doom-laden quotes running through his head. *The tradition of the dead generations weighs like a nightmare on the minds of the living.* That seemed to apply to the two families, Mansfield and Macmillan. His mind was spinning from all the upset and the chilling things he had learned, but increasingly his mind was spinning towards Charlotte. Charlotte was his centre of gravity amid the maelstrom. Inside his car, he put a call through to her, praying she would answer. She answered almost at once.

"What are you doing this evening?" he asked. He knew he didn't sound his usual self, but he couldn't help it.

"Remind me," she prompted.

He released a taut breath. "I need to unwind, Charlie. What say we walk around the city enjoying the lights? We can catch a meal somewhere."

"So what's happened now?" she asked, gently.

"You really are *too* intuitive." Her intuitions were part of what drew them so closely together.

"There's something you want to tell me. I hear it in your voice. Is it about your mother? She's dying to have me over for Christmas Day? Let the festive season roll, that sort of thing?"

"I'm not going anyway," Brendon said, rubbing a hand across his face.

"Gotcha," Charlotte replied. "I've had a great time too. I rang Uncle Conrad this afternoon to tell him I want him and Aunt Patricia to vacate Clouds by the end of January. I intend to use the house as my getaway."

"And of course he said he understood perfectly," Brendon said sarcastically. "He had his eye on another house anyway?"

"He could have said that, but most of what he yelled down the phone was incomprehensible. I did gather he wasn't very pleased."

"But he understood?"

"Rest easy, Bren, he did. I can crack a skull or two. Dare I mention that Sir Reginald Mansfield was my grandfather?"

Laughter rose in him, softening his mood. "I'll pick you up in an hour, okay?" He wanted to take a shower, cool down, and change his city clothes.

"Terrific. We can get off to a flying start."

Christmas is a time of celebration. It is also the time of the year when Sydney puts on a fantastic light show, with blues, pinks, violets, greens, and amethyst, using the façades of all its historic buildings, its iconic Opera House and Sydney Harbour Bridge, the world's tallest steel arch structure connecting the North Shore with the city centre. The bridge, spanning the magnificent harbour, a sparkling cobalt blue by day, couldn't have made a more advantageous site for thrilling displays of fireworks and light spectacles. The entire city was looking forward to the annual New Year's Eve midnight fireworks, arguably the best in the world.

That evening one of the best light spectacles and the largest crowd-drawer was the Catholic Cathedral, St Mary's, adjacent to beautiful Hyde Park with its playing fountains. The massive front façade of the cathedral, the tower, and its spires seventy-five metres high were illuminated with a changing display of Christmas themes, in lovely colours, the most beautiful of which, in Charlotte's opinion, were the iconic representations of Madonna and Child.

"I'd like to be married in St. Mary's," Charlotte found herself saying right out of the blue.

"You're not a Catholic, Charlie." Brendon looked down at her in surprise.

"They ought to open the cathedral doors to everyone. It seems to me religions don't bring people together, they set them apart, too often in terrible conflict. We hear about it every day. By the way, I've bought the Toohey Building. George Goss from Properties handled it for me."

"You don't fool around, do you?" he said, not altogether surprised. She had told him of her plans. "When did this happen?"

"Only today." Charlotte looked visibly delighted.

"I've never met anyone so young with so much focus as you,
Charlie," Brendon said.

"I'm not a dreamer, Bren," she said. "I have my dreams, but I
need to turn them into reality. All this money I've inherited, money I
don't *need*, has to benefit sections of the community who desperately
need help. I've been given the power to change things. I can make a
better life for a lot of deserving people, particularly women and children."

"Your heart is in the right place." He hugged her. "I'd tear the
building down. Start again."

"Precisely what I intend to do. We can go over the plans together
when they're ready. Our own architects can do the job. I'm going to
call it Lady Julia House."

"A lovely gesture." There was real feeling in Brendon's voice.
For a rich woman, or a woman married to an extremely rich man,
Lady Julia Mansfield's life had been in many ways a struggle. To
this day he didn't think Charlotte knew anything about Lady Julia's
connection to his grandfather.

"There's going to be plenty of security," Charlotte was saying.
"No enraged husbands or partners breaking in, threatening the
women there." She drew closer to him, taking his arm with girlish
enthusiasm. Multicoloured lights played across part of her face and
her glittering golden-blond hair. Tonight she was dressed casually in
a yellow silk camisole over white crop pants, a stylish pair of walking shoes on her feet. Brendon could feel her young body brushing
his own. Nothing could stand between them. He could feel his heart
beating in his chest. He could feel the pulse in his temple. He was
forced to the inevitable conclusion that he was in love with Charlotte.
Deeply in love with her, even though he could see all the turbulence
in front of them.

"You've something to tell me," she prompted, momentarily resting her head on his shoulder.

They were so close he could catch the essence of roses on her
skin. She had such delicate collarbones beneath her smooth skin. The
vee of her camisole top revealed the shadowed triangle between her

small, high breasts. His feeling for her by the day was becoming more and more intensely *physical*. He wanted to know every inch of her creamy flesh.

"Have I?" he stalled.

She laughed, the charming, musical sound he loved. "Of course you have," she said. "There's always a story to tell. I'd say your mother is very upset you're not having Christmas Day at the house?"

"That's not the least of it," he admitted. "When I left, pretty well punch-drunk from all I'd heard, my dad was only waiting to read the riot act."

"Perhaps he has waited overlong?" Charlotte suggested. "What started it? At a wild guess, something about me?" Charlotte's voice was almost lost in the laughter and chatter around them, the excited shrieks of children, the running around and clapping of their hands, as they revelled in the festive atmosphere.

"About you *and* your mother," Brendon told her. "Some of the things Dad had to say were shattering."

"He's been too noble about it all," Charlotte said, steadying a giggling toddler about to run into her. She held the child's shoulders gently until the young mother arrived with a breathless thank-you. "Jealousy must be a terrible burden to carry. It *is* one of the deadly sins. I expect your mother will hold to her beliefs until the day she dies. It must be painful indeed to love a man with all your heart and soul when you *know* he doesn't feel the same way about you."

"Unrequited love." Brendon nodded. "But my father has been very good to my mother. He's never strayed. There has never been any real instability in the marriage, when most marriages would have had their rough spots. My mother has everything she wants. Dad defers to her when I've always thought he shouldn't. Dad has had to carry a big burden too."

"We can't love on demand," Charlotte said, "though I suppose many couples do grow to love each other as they discover the good qualities in their partners. Your mother would be keen to see you married off to Lisa, who, I freely admit, is a fine choice. She's beautiful, intelligent, caring. A lovely woman, moreover, she loves you."

His answer was somewhat harsh. "As I've told you before, Charlotte, we have to close the book on Lisa. I don't love her. I never did tell her I loved her. Had I, I wouldn't have changed. Lisa is all the things you say, and I pray she finds the right man, but I want *more* from a woman. I want something that's going to last forever. Someone to share my life with, body and soul."

"And that's the whole of it, is it?" She tilted her glittering eyes to ask.

"Would you have it any other way?" he said in a deepening voice.

"No."

They turned into a handsome boulevard with long sparkling ropes of white lights strung overhead. The avenue was lined by bedecked real Christmas trees in huge glazed pots. "Would you like something to eat?" Brendon asked, concerned he was on the brink of giving himself away. He could see other young couples, stopping, kissing. He was swallowing the urge to do the same. Over and over and over. He needed the searing pleasure of having her in his arms.

"Coffee," Charlotte broke into his tortured thoughts. "Something chocolatey to go with it. I'm not actually hungry."

"Oddly enough, neither am I. Let's try Pascali's."

"Fine. The best coffee in town."

The warm and welcoming coffee shop was crowded, but Pascali himself organized a table for the two of them, wishing them both *Buon Natale* many times, with a kiss on both cheeks for Charlotte and a manly crush for Brendon, both of whom he knew well from their valued patronage.

Coffee duly arrived, accompanied by a platter of delectable little chocolate offerings. What both of them wanted really was some quiet time together, but who could tell what would happen? After that one kiss, their whole relationship had changed, no matter how much they sought to keep the old easy camaraderie on track. They spotted a few friends and acquaintances inside the coffee shop, all of whom were out for the evening doing what most of the city did, enjoying the wonderful spectacle of lights.

They were just rising to leave, when they literally ran into Lisa and another mutual friend, Shane Herrick. More greetings were exchanged, and a few pleasantries, but not before Charlotte caught the look on Lisa's lovely face. There was longing and regret, but for the very first time a visible green flash of jealousy in Lisa's eyes. Lisa had thought she and Brendon, although admittedly very close, were in no way romantically involved. It seemed as if Lisa had changed her mind.

Back on the boulevard Brendon warned, "I know what you're going to say. But don't say it."

"Gimme a break, I wasn't going to say a word. Shane isn't a bad catch. He's going really well in the advertising world. They say we get the people we deserve. Personally I don't believe that. Are we going home, by the way?"

"Where exactly is 'home'?" Brendon asked. "Your place or mine?"

Charlotte adopted a mock-pondering expression. "Mmmm . . . my place, I think. After all, you left the Porsche there."

It was impossible to find a cab, so they walked to Charlotte's Darling Point apartment, directly overlooking the harbour. Brendon's inner city apartment would have been the better choice. It was in striking distance. Neither of them minded the extended stroll, though. The breeze off the water was heavenly. It was a beautiful balmy Sydney summer night. The whole city was under the spell of Christmas. Although they had rarely held hands in the past they were holding hands now, neither with a thought of pulling away. Skin on skin was perfect. From the apartment complex someone was playing a song from an old Grace Kelly–Bing Crosby movie, *High Society.*

Bing's smooth, melodious Irish voice floated out over the brilliantly lit harbour, singing an ode to true love.

The crowd lining the area blazing with lights took the opportunity to join in. There were lots of kisses and loving embraces. The combined voices carried powerfully on the wind. Charlotte and Brendon, gripped by the joy of the moment, joined in. It was an extraordinary night filled with happiness not unmixed with nostalgia. Everyone had loved ones no longer with them, but never forgotten. Charlotte had more than her share of them. Wealth was no protection against the relentless hand of fortune.

Once inside the complex, the magic disappeared like a puff of smoke. Conrad and Patricia Mansfield, heads down, in the middle of a fierce argument, were charging out of the lift.

"I don't believe it!" was Brendon's laconic groan.

"Just what we're looking for," Charlotte said, never lost for words. "I had no idea they were coming into the city."

"No doubt they wanted to drop off your Christmas present," Brendon suggested.

Patricia Mansfield saw them first. "Charlotte, we wanted to see you," she announced loudly, her eyes sweeping over Brendon, who was looking incredibly handsome. "Only we couldn't wait any longer."

"A very Happy Christmas to you too, Aunt Patricia and Uncle Conrad. Why didn't you say you were coming into the city?"

"We're spending Christmas Day with the Carringtons," Patricia Mansfield said, as if the Carringtons were the crème de la crème. Which, in fact, they were. "I might have known we'd find the two of you together."

"And that's a problem?" Brendon retorted, very crisply indeed.

Patricia declined to answer. She couldn't take her eyes off of him. Everything about Brendon Macmillan threw her off balance.

"I wondered if I might have a word with you, Charlotte," Conrad Mansfield asked, his expression vaguely demonic.

"Surely you haven't left anything out?" Charlotte didn't bother to hide the sarcasm.

"I'd be obliged." Conrad's green eyes revealed a glimmer of anxiety.

"Okay, then. Come up. I hope it won't take long. Brendon and I are going out again, so many people to see, however briefly. There are parties going on all over Sydney."

Once inside Charlotte's beautiful, art-filled apartment, Patricia renewed her attack as though she didn't know any other way. "I suppose you know you broke up Simon's romance with Carol Sutton?" She shot a glance at Charlotte, her breathing fast and shallow.

"Did he tell you about it?" Brendon asked.

"He said nothing about it," Conrad broke in. "I expect it was all his fault. In my opinion, the girl has had a lucky break."

"By the time I arrived at Carol's flat, your splendid son, Aunt Patricia, had already given poor Carol a vicious backhander." Charlotte tackled the issue head-on. "She wanted to end the relationship, you see. Simon wasn't having that."

Patricia Mansfield stared in stunned indignation. "I *do . . . not . . .* believe you. Simon wouldn't dream of hitting a woman. It's unthinkable!"

"Actually, it happens in all sections of society," Charlotte said. "If Simon so much as gets within a few feet of Carol again, an AVO will be taken out against him."

Patricia was so genuinely shocked that she slumped into a plush armchair. "I cannot believe my son capable of such a cowardly act."

"Men are capable of anything," Charlotte said, dispassionately. "What is it you want to talk to me about, Uncle Conrad? It has to be important if you've spent some time waiting for us."

"You're always with her, aren't you, Brendon?" Patricia Mansfield gave a bitter laugh. "It's almost incestuous."

Brendon turned a little pale under his golden summer tan. "I deeply resent that, Mrs. Mansfield. I demand you retract it."

Conrad Mansfield looked at his wife reprovingly. "You're such a damned fool, Patricia. I knew I should have come on my own."

"I'm waiting," Brendon said, keeping his light-filled eyes on Patricia Mansfield.

Patricia shifted nervously under his brilliant regard. "I apologize, Brendon. I didn't mean anything by it. It's just you're always *there*." As she spoke, she was winding her magnificent diamond engagement ring 'round and 'round on her finger.

"Just as well, with people like your son hanging about," Brendon shot back tersely.

As they exchanged verbal blows, Conrad Mansfield began roaming the large, beautifully proportioned living room. Its great double doors of glass and steel Charlotte had had dressed up with archways, painted white like the walls. The colour scheme reflected the beautiful harbour environment, with blue, white, turquoise, and green around the room. On the broad terrace looking directly out at the glittering harbour, he could see masses of flowers cascading out of pots. There was a sitting area as well, outfitted with white wicker furniture. At one end of the room stood a very beautiful French boullework desk that had belonged to Lady Julia, his mother. His mother, too, had had style. Charlotte had inherited it, as well as the Old Man's steel. He moved down to the desk, appraising it before running his hand over the marquetry of engraved brass and tortoiseshell. He had coveted this desk, although it was a bit on the feminine side.

Charlotte stood watching her uncle. She was unconsciously holding her breath, like a woman suppressing some need to cry out. Shivers were running up and down her spine like icy fingers. The downlights were full on one side of her uncle's face, the other side was in shadow. His face wore an expression she had seen before, an avid, madly desirous expression. She had seen that exact expression a long time before. Her throat was dry. She found she couldn't swallow. Images began to emerge from the sunken depths of her memory. She was only twelve years old . . .

She walked into her father's study desperate for comfort, desperate for an image of her father she could cling to. Her parents were dead and laid to rest, but they were still very much alive to her. She had spent a great deal of time in her father's study. He had been the most indulgent of fathers, as indeed her grandfather had always treated her with kindness, gruff perhaps, but she was in no doubt that he loved her. No door in Clouds had been locked against her. She had been initiated into its secrets. She was Christopher's daughter—all that remained of him.

Inside the room, she found her uncle Conrad standing behind her father's desk, his handsome blond head bent over, his brow furrowed like he was studying something that held a peculiar and powerful fascination for him. He was so engrossed, turning page after page of a huge pile of papers, that for a moment he didn't even realize she was there. When he looked up, abruptly alerted, his avid expression was wiped clean. In its place was a chilling anger and a range of emotions she couldn't decipher. Whatever it was, it filled her with blind terror. She had every right to go into her father's study, yet her uncle utterly incomprehensibly began to thunder at her. "What are you doing here, Charlotte? Get out at once."

Charlotte stared back in astonishment. Her uncle had never spoken to her like that before. It would not have been tolerated. She was frightened by the great change in him, but she mustered the courage to point at him, her index finger outstretched as if in accusation. "What are you reading? What is it that you don't want me to see?" She had to let him know she was no fool.

Her uncle, as if in acknowledgement, took several steps from behind the desk, coming purposefully towards her. His nostrils were flaring. Here was a tall, strong man who looked like her father but could never be her father. This was a stranger projecting an infinite anger. She had seen menacing figures in movies who looked just like that. She knew what she had to do. She turned and ran, as if from an alien presence, truly frightened of the stranger's next move. Only she and her grandmother were at home, her grandmother a frail lady besieged by grief.

From that day on, she never said a word to anyone. Not even to herself. Her memories sank deeper and deeper. Only silence would protect her.

Nine years later Charlotte found herself falling right back into the moment when she thought her own uncle would attack her.

Brendon gave her a quick, concerned look. "Charlie, what is it?" She had lost colour. He watched her fall into an armchair, as if she felt faint.

"Charlie?" Brendon swiftly crossed the space that divided them, going down on his knees. "What is it? Are you all right?"

"I expect you've been drinking," Patricia Mansfield said by way of explanation, though she too had a startled expression in her eyes. "Buck up, Charlotte. Can I get you anything?"

Charlotte lifted her head. "Once the villain, always the villain, isn't that right, Uncle Conrad?" Her green eyes were locked on her uncle.

"Make sense, girl," he answered sharply, his features drawn so tight she could almost see the skeleton skull beneath.

"Everything has come together," she said, tapping her forehead. "That day in the study years ago. It wasn't all that long after the accident. Do you remember? I do *now*. You were pouring over a thick pile of papers you'd found in my father's study. You were racing through the pages, devouring them as you were being devoured. You were so intent on what you were reading—what you couldn't *believe* you were reading—that you didn't see me at first. Remember?"

"I have no recollection of that whatever," was Conrad Mansfield's curt reply.

"Allow me to help you out. I went into the study for some comfort. My father loved my company. I wanted his, even though he had been taken from me. You shouted at me to get out. You had never shouted at me before. Your face had turned into a terrible mask. It was bewildering, frightening. I didn't know who you were. I believed you meant to harm me."

Patricia Mansfield was squirming in her armchair. "I've never heard such fanciful nonsense in all my life." She was staring at Charlotte as though she had taken leave of her senses. "Your uncle would never hurt you, Charlotte. It would never even cross his mind. You were a traumatized child. I suspect you're describing a nightmare you had, that's all. I've had living nightmares myself."

"You want proof?" Charlotte asked quietly. "You haven't read the new manuscript as you claimed, Aunt Patricia. I think you were trying to reassure yourself as much as I was. There may be a new manuscript, but the opening page is drivel."

Conrad Mansfield's skin flushed with hot blood. "You think so?"

"I know so. Maybe it's the best you can do," Charlotte said. "You're not a real writer, Uncle Conrad. My father was the writer. He never said anything to anyone about it, but he had finished a novel he called *Cries of the Heart*. He had put it aside for the time being while he dealt with other problems, not the least of them the lies that were being spread about Brendon's father and my mother, but at some point he would have looked for a publisher. Only he was killed. You had no idea about the book, did you, Uncle Conrad? When you found it tucked away in the study, you knew you had uncovered a masterpiece. It was good enough to get short-listed for the Booker, which indeed it was. You were always looking for something to gain Grandfather's attention. I do understand how upsetting it must have been for you, living in your older brother's shadow. You thought about it and thought about it and concluded you were safe. I was always a risk, but you waited long enough to realize I had buried my memory of that day. That's what grief and fear can do."

Patricia Mansfield went to stand up, her legs so weak she had to fall down again. "I don't believe a word of this," she said, her whole body visibly shaking.

"It's like smashing a mirror only to find a devil on the other side," Brendon suggested. "You haven't read the new manuscript, have you?"

Patricia owned up. "Maybe I haven't, but I deplore Charlotte's accusation that her uncle, my husband, Simon's father, stole some work supposedly written by Christopher, just to crown himself with glory?"

"He played a very dangerous game," Brendon put forth his ominous opinion.

Patricia stared at him with glassy eyes. "I *know* my husband, Brendon. He is *not* a common thief. What would Simon say? He would be enormously upset by this accusation. He worships his father."

Charlotte was moved to contradict. "The only person Simon worships is himself. A mother should always protect her child, but a mother also has a duty to raise her child right. You weren't doing Simon any favours giving in to him at every turn. You turned him into a tyrant."

Patricia pulled a shocked face. "You're going too far, Charlotte."

"Do shut up, woman!" Conrad snarled, turning away from his wife to address Charlotte. "I've got a problem then?"

"You didn't write *Cries of the Heart,* did you?" Charlotte asked with sad disdain.

Her uncle's eyes bore into hers as though he could read her mind. He gave a terrible smile that was more a grimace of pain and humiliation. "You can see now why there has been no follow-up. I didn't write that book. Christopher did, though God knows how he found the time. I discovered it. I read it. I realized how very good it was. I bided my time, and then, when I deemed myself safe, I sent it on to my publishing house. They loved it. The rest is history. I can see what's left to me, Charlotte. You let it be known your father wrote *Cries of the Heart,* leaving me with no option but to end my life. The public humiliation, the uproar, the disgust of my publishers, it would be too much to endure. You may have noticed I'm far from a happy man. There are plenty of places for me to simply slip on the grassy verge and go over the cliff when out walking."

Charlotte left that threat aside for the moment. Her uncle was pretty good at emotional blackmail. She looked to her aunt, a woman seemingly turned to stone. "I want the truth now, Aunt Patricia. Lie and this could end more badly than it will already. Did you spread the vile rumours about my mother and Julian Macmillan?"

Patricia Mansfield looked as though she was about to be sick. She shook her head, one hand to her throat. "If I had done that, Charlotte, I would never have had a moment's peace. I admit I was very jealous of your mother. She was everything I'm not. But I wasn't the only one jealous of her, mind you. Brendon's mother, Olivia, the Ice Queen, positively *hated* her. I swear to you, I was as shocked by the rumours as everyone else. I confess I thought, well, that there's no smoke without fire. Not my finest hour. I never saw one instance when either Alyssa or Julian behaved improperly or even suspiciously. What am I anyway, a traitor? I might have been jealous of Alyssa, but Christopher was always charming to me. He treated me with respect."

"Perhaps it was your sainted mother, Brendon?" Conrad suggested unpleasantly. "I wouldn't dismiss the possibility. We all know Olivia has an obsessive nature."

For a moment Brendon felt despair. He responded carefully, "Did you come forward with your suspicions?"

"Good heavens no!" Conrad glowered. "As far as I was concerned, the two of them could live in hell for a while, but I never wished tragedy upon them. So, what's the verdict, Charlotte? You're going to throw me to the wolves, thinking I'll do the decent thing and throw myself off the mountain?"

Charlotte brushed a gleaming lock of hair from her face. There were so many things wrong with her uncle. "Save the emotional blackmail," she said. "I don't believe you could end your own life, anyway. You don't have the guts. Destroying people is not my thing, and consequently I could never publicly humiliate you for one reason only. You're *family*, such as it is. It would impact severely on Simon's career, if he's ever going to take one up. It would ruin Aunt Patricia's social life. I'm sure a forensics team would find my father's fingerprints on your masterpiece. I require the original manuscript. It's mine."

Conrad Mansfield's chest appeared to cave in. "And even if you're true to your word, what about Macmillan here? He'd point the finger at me at a moment's notice."

"So I would," Brendon freely admitted, "if you weren't Charlotte's uncle. It's her decision. I back her. Bad publicity has its impact even on the innocent. You might spare a thought for what your *wife* may do, sir? She looks stunned by what she's hearing."

Conrad shrugged, not even bothering to look at his wife. "No need to worry about Patricia. She puts Simon first in everything. You'd think he was a wonderful, idealistic young man likely to make prime minister, instead of a would-be waster and a woman beater who's not coming up to her high hopes. If my dear wife attempts to destroy me, she'll be destroying our son as well. That will never happen."

"What do you say to that, Mrs. Mansfield?" Brendon asked, trying to remain courteous. It was obvious Patricia had never doubted her husband had produced *Cries of the Heart.* He felt pity. Patricia Mansfield, always so self-righteous, looked perilously close to collapse.

She did sit dumbly for a moment, and then she delivered her intentions. "I will not put my son in danger. Simon is the love of my life. I don't understand why, but I don't wish to push my husband beyond his limits. He could well end his own life. I'm being serious here, Charlotte?" Patricia shot Charlotte a desperate glance. "Conrad has a very poor view of himself. He grew up that way. He will never change. I loved him when I married him. I can't say I love him now, but he is still my husband, the father of my son. The Mansfields as a family have to stick together."

Charlotte couldn't allow that to pass. "What a difference it would have made had you acted on that ideal nine years ago, Aunt Patricia. You kept me out in the cold."

"I had to," Patricia confessed, looking ashamed. "It was Conrad who didn't want you around. Now I know why. I expect he was terrified you'd remember."

"The deaths of my mother and father left me traumatized. I needed to forget that day in the study to survive. Only recently little lights have been going on and off in my brain. I've always wondered why I felt fear of you, Uncle. Now we know."

"I would never have hurt you, Charlotte. I would die first." Conrad threw her a look that was more arrogant than pleading. "You must believe that."

"Sorry, Uncle, I don't," Charlotte said. "You would have had me stopped one way or another. I'm sure of it."

"No, Charlotte, *no!*" Patricia protested, but not in her usual emphatic fashion.

"I hope you realize the mercy Charlotte is showing?" Brendon's tone was condemning.

"Conrad doesn't deserve it, but Simon does," Patricia cried, a loyal mother if nothing else. "I thank you from the bottom of my heart, Charlotte. God knows what Sir Reginald would have done. Conrad would be swinging from a tree somewhere, I suspect."

"I don't know about that, but my uncle would have known soon enough. So we're all agreed?" Charlotte asked.

"We are." Husband and wife spoke as one. Obviously they had concluded that was the only way to go.

"First things first," Brendon broke in. "Charlotte wants her father's manuscript back ASAP. It will be safely locked away."

"I'll hand it to her myself," Conrad Mansfield promised, his green eyes gone lifeless.

"Finally, Charlotte wants you to vacate Clouds by the end of January. That should be sufficient time. Please do not attempt to take anything that doesn't belong to you."

Charlotte relented. "If you want a special piece, Aunt Patricia, you have only to ask me," she said. Bitterness and resentment only served to corrode the soul. She didn't want that. "I'll be installing caretakers, but I'll be using the house frequently for various purposes. I mean to reopen the rose gardens to the public, to make them accessible just as Grandma did. You might consider a stint in the south of France, Uncle Conrad, to regain your composure. You could even decide to settle there. It's entirely up to you."

"Time for those two to face up to reality," Charlotte said as she closed the door on her uncle and aunt after watching them move off heavily to the lift.

Brendon found his heart was thrashing about in his chest. He had no time for the Mansfields. He was thinking more about his own family. It had been his hope that Charlotte would never find out about his mother and the part she had played in the disastrous rift between Alyssa and Christopher. His mother had set aside all conscience to bring Alyssa down like some beautiful bird on the wing. Only Charlotte would drive through to the truth. She wouldn't stop until she did. He had to break it to her first, but there was no way of breaking it to her gently.

Charlotte was staring at him as though she knew what was going through his mind. "I've never heard your mother described as the 'Ice Queen' before, have you?"

"First time I've heard it," he said. At least that was true. Conrad Mansfield, despicable man that he was, had managed to hit the nail on the head.

"Two mysteries were solved here tonight," Charlotte said. "My father wrote *Cries of the Heart*. Isn't that wonderful? It will come out one day. I'm determined on that. Second, Aunt Patricia wasn't the one to spread the rumours. I believed her, did you?"

"I did," Brendon said grimly.

"I never considered your mother, who has always lived such an exemplary life." Suddenly Charlotte felt such intense fear she had difficulty speaking another word.

All that stood between them was the electric air. Brendon had to defend his mother no matter what she had done. "Why fix on my mother?" he asked. "There are other interpretations."

Charlotte moved to where Brendon was standing, staring up into his face. Her emerald eyes were blazing. "Because everything has come to a head, Bren," she said. "Your parents and mine, my uncle and aunt, they are all of a generation. They knew one another well. I don't like the label 'Ice Queen' any more than you do, but I'm worried by the way you look. I feel the pain in you. I see the haunted expression. Something you learned this evening has greatly upset you. It's not just your mother wanting me out of your life. That's always been her attitude, but you've never taken any notice before. You've always been far more loyal to me than her."

"I don't want to lose you, Charlotte," Brendon said, beginning to turn away. "I should be going."

In an instant she was in front of him, quick as a gazelle. She blocked the door, launching the accusation at him like a missile. "It *was* your mother, wasn't it? Wasn't it, Bren?"

There was no right answer. None.

When he didn't speak, she hit him hard in the chest. It might have been a stab from a sword.

"Did that holier-than-thou, gold-plated woman explain to you she was out of her mind with jealousy? Was that it?"

He didn't evade the truth. He stood stoically, accepting what was to come. "Yes, it was."

"Bren!" White to the lips, not really knowing what she was doing, Charlotte lifted an aching, trembling arm, her fingers outspread. Her whole body was struggling to control the primitive urges that were taking her over. Her whole existence had been clouded by lies. Brendon, her hero, had shattered her feelings.

He caught her hand by the wrist, holding it aloft. "Do all you Mansfields lash out?" he asked in a cutting voice. He caught her to him, lifting her off her feet. She weighed nothing, but he wanted every bit of her. "I love you, Charlotte," he said. "Of all the women in the world, I love you, but I want to be on my way."

"Coward!" Her green eyes were fierce upon him.

He let her drop to her feet, like a kitten. "*What* did you say?"

A powerful energy was coming off of him, a male domination her body recognized. "I called you a coward," she repeated.

Passion was coming down on Brendon in hammering waves. It was like being caught in a tide that didn't know how or where to stop. There were rules in life. A son always defended his mother. On the other hand, the links to Charlotte were so strong he might have been fused to her through all time. He pulled her into him, his fingers spearing through her thick, springy waves and curls as he held up her face to him. His love for her was unrivalled, as was the pleasure she gave him. She appeared to be having her struggles, too. Her full, tender mouth was parted on a cry of wry melancholy. "Aaah, Bren! It's all too terrible."

"I know." Instinctively he gathered her closer, one hand caressing her body. "I acknowledge the terrible wrong."

"*Wrong?* She isn't just the Ice Queen, she's the Enemy Queen."

"Please stop, Charlotte," he begged.

"Then stop me. Make your move."

He didn't hesitate. His mouth came down over hers, covering it with the mastery that shut off all further words, and flushed Charlotte's entire body in heat. It was a kiss that grew deeper and deeper, a kiss charged with hunger. Brendon told himself it was always going to end this way. They were fated to be lovers. Neither of them was content with the relationship that had lasted through childhood into the present with all its temptations. "I love you, Charlotte," he said, shoving aside their problems as though they didn't exist.

She was silent within the circle of his arms. One of the straps of her yellow camisole had fallen off her slender shoulder. He pushed the other one off. Too late to stop him. It only took another movement of his hand for the silk top to fall to her waist. She was wearing a pretty little scrap of a bra. He released that too, his hands closing with a kind of ecstasy over her warm, naked breasts. The rose-pink of her nipples were peaking against his palms. She was aroused, for all her terrible upset.

All that existed was desire. It overrode every other consideration. Still she didn't speak. She didn't try to wriggle out of his grasp. What was driving him was driving her, a leaping flame intent on bringing about their surrender.

Charlotte lifted her arms, locked them tightly around his neck. "You love me? *Show* me," she whispered fiercely. "Show me how much you love me. That's the first and last time I'll ask you."

"Is it really?" A fire blazed in him. "A woman born to give orders."

"Are you up to that?" she challenged.

He locked her seamlessly to him. "This is no *game* we're playing, Charlotte."

"I'm not into games, Bren."

"What if you fall pregnant? I'm not so far gone I can't consider that."

"You wouldn't want our child?" she taunted him.

Their child! At the thought, a high rapture rose in him. He knew he could be a good father. Charlotte loved children. "Don't be ridiculous, Charlie," he said. "You're my everything and you know it, but you have to be entirely *free*. Free to choose the who, the where, and the when."

"Then I *have* chosen. I choose *you*, Brendon Macmillan. I choose you, despite your family. It might be sooner than expected, but maybe we're simply wasting time not being together. Have you thought of that? I love you, Bren. I trust you. I need you by my side. I need your brains, your advice, your high principles, your strength, and your loyalty, not to mention your love. You're perfect to me."

An enormous load lifted clear off his shoulders. Despite everything, Charlotte chose him. There was a future. "As you are to me."

"Naturally I've taken precautions," she confided. "I'm nobody's wild child."

He broke off what he was doing, which was trailing kisses down her arched throat. "You conniving little minx."

"Thank you." Charlotte took it as a compliment. "There's a lot of work to be done before we can think of a family." She stared up at him as though the whole world was waiting with bated breath for his response.

"Meanwhile we have tonight to celebrate." There was tragedy. There were tears, sadness, and recriminations. Perhaps even a touch of evil. But the future belonged to him and Charlotte. He swept her off her feet, holding her high in his arms. "I mean to show you, Charlotte, what a man's love for his woman is like."

"As soon as possible," Charlotte said.

A dazzle of light was coming from her bedroom, spilling out onto the carpeted corridor. A moment later Brendon laid Charlotte down on the bed, where she remained motionless, staring up at him with glistening emerald eyes. Without taking his gaze off her, Brendon began stripping off his clothes, pausing for a moment to say, "I believe I should propose to you first."

Charlotte broke into a beautiful, joyful peal of laughter. "Please, please do," she begged. "We're going to change everything, aren't we, Bren?"

"Everything except our love for each other." Naked, the light playing off his fine tanned skin, Brendon went down on one knee, reaching for her hand. What he saw made him ask worriedly, "Charlie, why are you crying?"

"Don't you see?" Charlotte leaned over to plant a dewy wet kiss on his mouth. "I'm so *happy!*"

"Thank God for that! I mean for you to grow happier with every single day. You *will* do as I now ask. Will you marry me?" His silver-grey eyes shone brilliantly on her face.

"I will," Charlotte said as solemnly as if she were making a sacred vow. Then unexpectedly she began to laugh again. "Can you really see me marrying anyone else?"

"Not after tonight you won't," said Brendon, rising to his feet.

He looked down at her, the coverlet she was lying on gleamed like some gloriously inviting stretch of sand. Charlotte remained motionless, her golden hair a halo around her head, her emerald eyes full of glittering lights. Those extraordinary jewel-like glints spoke of her desire for him, serving to increase his own ardour.

Before he got completely carried away by feelings of love and longing, he turned to switch off the overhead lights, leaving only one softly glowing lamp. Radiant moonlight streamed into the room with the city lights adding a whole spectrum of glowing colour to the silvery-white. The bedroom seemed to carry the scent of all the flowers in the world. It was the scent of her, he realized. He was breathing in her fragrance, her warmth, her very breath that had the freshness of citrus.

As he bent over her to take her mouth, her body rose up to meet him, her beautiful head thrown back, soft sweet moans coming from her parted lips.

"Bren?" There was agitation in the depths of her voice, mixed with wonder. "Come to me," she pleaded.

"I'm coming." His heart was hammering as the level of intimacy built and bonded them.

Charlotte repeated his name over and over as if she loved it when he was there beside her. When he was kissing her deeply inside her yearning mouth.

He started making love to her, gently gliding his hands all over her body, lingering over its soft curves and clefts that were lightly beaded with perspiration from the burning heat inside her. She twisted easily this way and that, her spine liquid, her breasts swelling from the tenderness of his mouth and fingertips. This was really happening to her. This was what she had been waiting for. Brendon, her beautiful Brendon. Her lover.

They kissed light and fast, long and hard. They kissed deeply, intoxicated by the pleasure. It made Charlotte excited and breathless, poised on the brink, yet anchored by Brendon's strong arms. She understood perfectly the miraculous power of sex with the right man. She was pinned beneath him, her long slender legs trembling, her breath coming in little rasps. She arched her back, her legs rising of their own accord to lock around his waist. Her thighs were fused to his in that single action. They were almost . . . almost . . . one. The pleasure was so intense she was moaning aloud, her breath catching as he penetrated the inner lips of her quivering flesh.

It was both an ecstasy and an agony for Brendon. He had to control the fierceness of his longing. Charlotte was a virgin. The penetration of her body needed to be gradual, causing no pain but a delicious tingling.

Very quickly they found their perfect rhythm. Both were preparing themselves for the ravenous climax that was surely coming. It built to a crescendo that was near frightening, it had so much power, agonizing, full of a primal rapture. When the moment came, Charlotte's body was as tight as a high tension wire before shattering into a wild release that was pure ecstasy. Her fists beat helplessly against the body of her lover, the sounds coming out of her throat sounds that had never come out of her before. She belonged with Brendon and no one else.

It was quite a time after before Charlotte came to her senses. They lay, their bodies entwined. Brendon's strong chest was moving up and down, his heart kicking against his ribs. What had happened between them was like passing through fire that was supernaturally empowering.

Charlotte lay murmuring against his shoulder, her voice low and throaty. "We go together, don't we, Bren?" she said. "Like the sun and the moon, the earth and the trees." There was such euphoria in her voice it made his heart soar. "I love you, Brendon. Love you. Love you. Love you."

He pressed her ever closer to him. "And you are the very best thing that has ever happened to me, Charlotte. I worship you from the tip of your beautiful gold head to your twinkling toes. You are the one and only woman for me."

"I agree." She kissed him tenderly.

He took her hand in his, discovering he was wanting her yet again. They had all night. They had the promise of a blessed life.

Julian Macmillan was sitting quietly alone in the library. It was filled with golden light from a matching pair of Chinese blue and white vases mounted as lamps. The light gleamed on the paintings on the walls, the gold tooling on all the leather-bound books. His father's diplomas, his, and Brendon's, all had been framed with highly polished ebony borders. They too found a place. The Macmillan clan, like the Mansfields, was a highly successful, highly dysfunctional family.

He sat nursing an excellent cognac. It was his third. He wasn't going anywhere. From time to time, he gave vent to a deep sigh. Christmas Eve and here he was, the very picture of despondency. He felt as though his marriage had finally come to the end of the line. Regrets were uppermost in his mind. Especially the regret that he had not won Alyssa's hand before his friend Christopher had even laid eyes on her. In any case, Alyssa had truly loved Christopher. Whenever they met face-to-face, without any witnesses, his and Alyssa's conversation had a warm quality to it, but the content could have been overheard by anyone. It was very possible that a woman like

Alyssa had sensed his true feelings for her, but she had handled their relationship with grace and aplomb as he imagined he had. She was Christopher's wife. He was Christopher's best friend.

When he met Olivia, he had thought he could find happiness with this strikingly elegant, well-bred young woman who was clearly attracted to him. In the early days, he had been encouraged to think the happiness he had missed out on would start to flow. Olivia had offered herself to him completely. She was a fine hostess. She took a great interest in his professional life. She bore him the love of their lives, their son. It should have worked, only something terrible and mysterious happened. Olivia, literally overnight, was seized by her first violent attack of jealousy.

Since wedding Olivia, he had taken the utmost steps to appear totally devoted to his wife, which in the main, he was. Only that one evening when he and Alyssa had been talking on the terrace after one of Olivia's dinner parties, Olivia had casually looked out through the bay window to where he and Alyssa were standing quietly, perhaps overlong?

Whatever Olivia had spotted on her radar, from that evening on she had changed. There had been no jealous tears, no discussion, certainly no accusation, but it was made clear to him that Olivia understood his feelings, however well hidden, for the wife of his lifelong friend. There was no outward unpleasantness, but Olivia's smiles had become rare. What smiles she had were reserved for their son.

On the surface, everything went on as before. In spite of her many skills, Olivia, who had started off well, lost her first flush of popularity. As for him, there was always the unspoken insinuation that he was . . . well, a traitor. Alyssa and Christopher were no longer in her good graces. Indeed, Olivia could never hear Alyssa's name without sharply moving off. Since that fateful evening, there had been no real communication between them. He buried himself in his work. Olivia slipped off her pedestal to start the vicious round of rumours that he and Alyssa Mansfield had been carrying on a secret affair.

She had then established the right to accuse him of monstrous behaviour, of disgracing them, when *she* was the one who had in secret dishonoured them all. As far as he was concerned, Olivia would never get her honour back. Even after the fatal accident on the mountain, Olivia had clung to her paranoia. Her pathological jealousy of Alyssa, instead of dissolving in a wave of guilt, had fallen on Alyssa's daughter, the twelve-year-old Charlotte.

His son had set himself up as the young girl's champion. They seemed to play the parts of close cousins, only they weren't. It was inevitable that the quality of their relationship would pass from close friends to the romantic love that was waiting for them on the other side.

He had made it very clear to his wife that he would not tolerate any effort on her part to drive a wedge between the young people. Not that she could, Julian thought. That would be attempting the impossible. There was a passionate honesty to Brendon. At least one Macmillan would find the happiness that had eluded him, he thought. As well as had eluded his father, Hugo, when Sir Reginald had stolen Julia away from right under his nose.

Julian was so lost in his thoughts he didn't notice his wife slip into the darkened room.

"May I speak to you, Julian?" Olivia asked from the open doorway.

He didn't turn his head. "We can't go on at this rate, Olivia. I thought I made that very clear."

"I can't give a good account for my past, Julian," Olivia said passionately, "but I love you. I've always loved you. Love made me do it."

"I think you mean *possessiveness* made you do it," Julian said, the tone of his voice driving the point home. "That's quite different from love, my dear."

"Please, may I sit down?" Olivia's voice quavered, and she seemed genuinely distressed.

Julian waved her into an armchair. "What is it you want to say?"

"Ah, well . . ." Olivia drifted into an armchair close by, a tall, elegant figure in an expensive ivory silk nightdress and matching robe, her hair caught up by a Spanish comb. "You and Brendon are all that matters to me in this world, Julian. I couldn't live without you."

Julian put up a staying hand. "No emotional blackmail, if you please, Olivia. It won't work. Not anymore. Whatever you chose to do is on your head, not mine."

"But I'm not trying to blackmail you, Julian," Olivia exclaimed. "That would be detestable."

"I'm glad you finally realize it," he said with great irony. "Lying to yourself is equally as detestable."

Olivia bowed her lustrous dark head in shame. "I've hurt you terribly, haven't I?"

"You've hurt yourself more," Julian retorted. "What you will *not* be doing is hurting our son. In hurting him, you'll be hurting Charlotte. They're madly in love, in case you haven't noticed?"

Olivia made a muffled sound. "How could they keep it from me, Julian? I'm Brendon's mother. Of course I know he loves her."

Julian almost started out of his chair. "Her... *he*... Her name is Charlotte. For God's sake, can't you say it?"

"*Charlotte!*" Olivia cried. "All right, Julian, I accept that I destroyed her mother's life."

"Don't forget Christopher's," Julian added bleakly.

"I've been begging God's forgiveness every night of my life," Olivia claimed.

"Then you'll have to beg harder," Julian advised.

"Oh, I will, I will! I promise you, I will." It was a plea for mercy. "I can't lose you, Julian. You should have confronted me years ago. It might have brought me to my senses. I knew I appeared dreadfully dull to you compared to Alyssa, and now her daughter, Charlotte. I lack charm. I always have. My own mother told me that from an early age. In fact, she told me that constantly. She even told me once I should have been a nun. When I think about it now, I realize she was very harsh with me. I grew up thinking that I lacked any womanly grace. I couldn't believe it when you looked my way. My mother told me I wouldn't get far, but I did. You married me. You treated me like I was precious to you, especially after Brendon was born. I tried, I really tried, Julian, to overcome my jealousy of Alyssa—a woman who had all the charm and the vitality I lacked. It was my mother, you know, who first pointed out your attraction to Alyssa."

Julian gripped the arms of his chair, his heart dilating. "*Louise* did?" His voice revealed his shock. He turned fully to his wife, his expression one of deep and grave amazement. His late mother-in-law, Louise, had been a handsome, coolly manipulative woman, but he hadn't thought her to be cruel. She had always been very pleasant to him. Olivia, on the surface so aloof and apparently self-assured, was in reality a deeply vulnerable, damaged woman. Her mother,

Louise, could well have made her what she had become. He had gone along thinking his wife and his mother-in-law were very close. They had been, but not apparently in the best, most harmonious way. "Did your mother know it was you who started the rumours?" he asked, his blood curdling in his veins.

Olivia averted her face. "She must have known, although we never talked about it. She altered quite a bit after the ... accident. She stayed away. Do you remember?"

He did. They had seen Louise less and less. "So your mother never gave you any help to overcome your jealousy, as a good mother would?"

Olivia's mouth twisted painfully. "You'd think your mother would be the one person you could always count on. You could go to her, tell her everything, and she would understand. Better yet, she would assist you in following her good advice. It never happened to me. I know it has never occurred to you, but my mother never complimented me on my dress, how I ran the house, or the good job I made of entertaining. She never told me I made you a good wife. She never once told me she was proud of me like my father did. Thank God he was there. I think it might have been hard for her seeing me married to such a successful, handsome man. From relative obscurity I became Mrs. Julian Macmillan. A psychiatrist might analyse my mother's state of mind and conclude she had a deeply jealous nature, which she handed on."

Julian tried to step back in time. "Why have you never told me any of this, Olivia? I would have known how to handle your mother."

"I was too ashamed," Olivia said with stark truth. "You know I've never had a close female friend to talk to. Other women recognize the dark in me. I know they've found my company increasingly off-putting."

"That could all change, Olivia," Julian said, pity in his heart. "It's odd you allowed your mother to convince you that you were a person of little value. It's simply not true. I always complimented you on your skills and talents. Your good looks have never been in question, either. You're a very stylish woman."

Olivia's eyes were great dark pools. "Would you give me another chance, Julian?" she begged. "I swear you won't regret it. I'll make friends with Charlotte. God knows she's an admirable young woman. I will start making amends with her tomorrow, as I beg her to forgive me. You can trust me, Julian. Truly you can. I will never repeat my mistakes of the past. I've learned a bitter lesson. I've made you unhappy. If you want a divorce, I'll give it to you. You deserve some happiness."

"I don't want a divorce, Olivia," Julian said, realizing, despite everything, it was true. "All I want is for things to change, to become easier. I want *you* to be happy. Your mother is dead and gone now. She can't hurt you anymore."

"Would you hold my hand?" Olivia begged in a mere thread of a voice.

"Come here to me," her husband said.

Life was a gamble, but sometimes it was worth the risk.

Epilogue

Inside the church, with its soaring archways and domed ceiling, the atmosphere, alight with the wonderful entrance music, was thrumming with anticipation. This was after all the wedding of the year; the union of two of the country's most illustrious families, the Macmillans and the Mansfields. The interior of the beautiful church was more spacious than most, was packed out with guests resplendent in their wedding finery. From the delighted faces and the soft, happy buzz of conversation they were thrilled to be here on this most auspicious occasion.

At the front of the church facing the flower-bedecked altar, Dr. Aidan Armstrong, Brendon's best man, whispered to his friend. "Your bride looks glorious, Bren. Take a quick look!"

Brendon was fairly wild to do so. He eased back, turning his dark head. His first thought? The image of Charlotte on their wedding day would be forever indelibly stamped on his mind. She was moving, *floating* down the red carpeted aisle on the arm of his grandfather, Sir Hugo Macmillan. His grandfather was beaming with pride. He was impeccably dressed—the dress code was formal—and still looking handsome and vigorous being blessed with good health.

They were passing pew after pew, sumptuously decorated by his mother with broad white satin and taffeta ribbons and sprigs of exquisite white Thai orchids embellished with tiny delicate green ferns. His mother had taken over the decoration of the church along with her bevy of helpers with Charlotte's full approval. Olivia Macmillan was an elegant and artistic woman. She was looking exceptionally chic on the day in a designer two piece outfit, top and long skirt in her favourite shade of sapphire blue. Sapphires flashed at her ears and throat. It was a great joy and relief to Brendon his mother had from the very start of the New Year accepted Charlotte with open arms, as his fiancée and as his future wife. He had been praying for a miracle. That miracle had happened. The once warring families were now reconciled, perfectly at peace.

His bride was drawing closer and closer, a creature of ethereal beauty, grace, and light. The sumptuous ivory silk of her strapless gown gleamed. From time to time the silk was shot through with colour as she passed by the magnificent stained glass windows. The tiny waist of her wedding gown was cinched tight. Flashes of light bounced off the gown's exquisite crystal beading and embroidery. Because of her petite stature, Charlotte was wearing a short, shimmering veil. It was held in place by her grandmother Lady Julia Mansfield's treasured bandeau that had come through Lady Julia's own family. The bandeau had a charming, not overwhelming medieval look to it that suited Charlotte beautifully. It was set with diamonds, pearls, and oval shaped emeralds. In her hands Charlotte carried a posy of the most perfect white roses from Clouds' home garden.

Behind her came her four smiling bridesmaids. Each was wearing a long strapless silk gown in the colour of the bride's favourite roses; exquisite pink, lovely lilac, creamy yellow and the very special moonlit blue of Blue Moon roses. All four bridesmaids wore their long gleaming hair sliding down their backs. They had been growing their hair for months for this great occasion. All four wore around their necks circlets of high quality semi-precious stones chosen to enhance the colour of their gowns. These had been presented to the bridesmaids by the groom as mementoes of this very special day.

The sight of his bride and the thrilling swell of the organ played by a master were making Brendon feel highly susceptible to overwhelming emotion. He knew many of the guests' eyes would be glazed over with tears. He understood that perfectly, just as he understood his role was to be the proud, smiling, confident groom ready to welcome his beautiful bride. Glorious sensations shot through him as Charlotte reached his side. There was a little smile on her lovely mouth, faintly teasing, but radiant, full of emotion. Her emerald eyes outdid the splendour of the precious emeralds in the bandeau that fixed her short white veil to her head. Her chief bridesmaid stepped up to take her bouquet. His grandfather stood back as Brendon took his bride's hand. It was trembling slightly so he increased a strong loving pressure, letting her know he would always be the protective force in her life.

As they turned together, Bishop Quentin Ainsworth, long known to both bride and groom, began the traditional ceremony. The Bishop was utterly confident these two fine young people would hold steadfast to their vows. Behind the young couple the church fell into an awed silence. Most of the guests thought they would never again in their lifetimes attend such a beautiful, harmonious wedding where bride and groom were so manifestly in love.

USA Today
Bestselling Author

MARGARET
WAY

*Even paradise
has its secrets...*

POINCIANA
ROAD

Please turn the page for an exciting peek at

Poinciana Road

by

Margaret Way!

Available in November 2016 at

your favourite bookstores and e-tailers.

Chapter 1

Mallory knew the route to Forrester Base Hospital as well as she knew the lines on the palms of her hands. She had never had the dubious pleasure of having her palm read, but she had often wondered whether palmistry was no more than superstition, or if there was something to it. Her life line showed a catastrophic break, and one had actually occurred. If she read beyond the break, she was set to receive a card from the Queen when she turned one hundred. As it was, she was twenty-eight. There was plenty of time to get her life in order and find some happiness. Currently her life was largely devoted to work. She allowed herself precious little free time. It was a deliberate strategy. Keep on the move. Don't sit pondering over what was lodged in the soul.

The driver of the little Mazda ahead was starting to annoy her. He was showing excessive respect for the speed limit, flashing his brake lights at every bend in the road. She figured it was time to pass, and was surprised when the driver gave her a loud honk for no discernible reason. She held up her hand, waved. A nice little gesture of camaraderie and goodwill.

She was almost there, thank the Lord. The farther she had travelled from the state capital, Brisbane, the more the drag on her emotions. That pesky old drag would never go away. It was a side effect of the baggage she carted around and couldn't unload. It wasn't that she didn't visualize a brave new world. It was just that so far it hadn't happened. Life was neither kind nor reasonable. She knew that better than most. She also knew one had to fight the good fight even when the chances of getting knocked down on a regular basis were high.

It had been six years and more since she had been back to her hometown. She wouldn't be returning now, she acknowledged with a stab of guilt, except for the unexpected heart attack of her uncle Robert. Her uncle, a cultured, courtly man, had reared her from age seven. No one else had been offering. Certainly not her absentee father, or her maternal grandparents, who spent their days cruising the world on the *Queen Mary 2.* True, they did call in to see her whenever they set foot on dry land, bearing loads of expensive gifts. But sadly they were unable to introduce a child into their busy lives. She was the main beneficiary of their will. They had assured her of that; a little something by way of compensation. She was, after all, their only grandchild. It was just at seven, she hadn't fit into their lifestyle. Decades later she still didn't.

Was it any wonder she loved her uncle Robert? He was her superhero. Handsome, charming, well off. A bachelor by choice. Her dead mother, Claudia, had captured his heart long ago when they were young and deeply in love. Her mother had gone to her grave with her uncle's heart still pocketed away. It was an extraordinary thing and in many ways a calamity, because Uncle Robert had never considered snatching his life back. He was a lost cause in the marriage stakes. As was she, for that matter.

To fund what appeared on the surface to be a glamorous lifestyle, Robert James had quit law to become a very popular author of novels of crime and intrigue. The drawing card for his legions of fans was his comedic detective, Peter Zero, never as famous as the legendary Hercule Poirot, but much loved by the readership.

Pulp fiction, her father, Nigel James, Professor of English and Cultural Studies at Melbourne University, called it. Her father had always stomped on his older brother's talent. "Fodder for the ignorant masses to be read on the train." Her father never minced words, the crueller the better. To put a name to it, her father was an all-out bastard.

It was Uncle Robert who had spelled love and a safe haven to her. He had taken her to live with him at Moonglade, his tropical hideaway in far North Queensland. In the infamous "blackbirding" days, when South Sea islanders had been kidnapped to work the Queensland cane fields, Moonglade had been a thriving sugar plantation. The house had been built by one Captain George Rankin, who had at least fed his workers bananas, mangoes, and the like and paid them a token sum to work in a sizzling hot sun like the slaves they were.

Uncle Robert had not bought the property as a working plantation. Moonglade was his secure retreat from the world. He could not have chosen a more idyllic spot, with two listed World Heritage areas on his doorstep: the magnificent Daintree Rainforest, the oldest living rainforest on the planet, and the glorious Great Barrier Reef, the world's largest reef system.

His heart attack had come right out of the blue. Her uncle had always kept himself fit. He went for long walks along the white sandy beach, the sound of seagulls in his ears. He swam daily in a brilliantly blue sea, smooth as glass. To no avail. The truth was, no one knew what might happen next. The only certainty in life was death. Life was a circus; fate the ringmaster. Her uncle's illness demanded her presence. It was her turn to demonstrate her love.

Up ahead was another challenge. A procession of undertakers? A line of vehicles was crawling along as though they had all day to get to their destination. Where the heck *was* that? There were no shops or supermarkets nearby, only the unending rich red ochre fields lying fallow in vivid contrast with the striking green of the eternal cane. Planted in sugarcane, the North was an area of vibrant colour and great natural beauty. It occurred to her the procession might be heading to the cemetery via the South Pole.

Some five minutes later she arrived at the entrance to the hospital grounds. There was nothing to worry about, she kept telling herself. She had been assured of that by none other than Blaine Forrester, who had rung her with the news. She had known Blaine since her childhood. Her uncle thought the world of him. Fair to say Blaine was the son he never had. She *knew* she came first with her uncle, but his affection for Blaine, five years her senior, had always ruffled her feathers. She was *more* than Blaine, she had frequently reminded herself. He was the only son of good friends and neighbours. She was *blood*.

Blaine's assurances, his review of the whole situation, hadn't prevented her from feeling anxious. In the end Uncle Robert was all the family she had. Without him she would be alone.

Entirely alone.

The main gates were open, the entry made splendid by a pair of poincianas in sumptuous scarlet bloom. The branches of the great shade trees had been dragged down into their perfect umbrella shape by the sheer weight of the annual blossoming. For as far back as she could remember, the whole town of Forrester had waited for the summer flowering, as another town might wait for an annual folk festival. The royal poinciana, a native of Madagascar, had to be the most glorious ornamental tree grown in all subtropical and tropical parts of the world.

"Pure magic!" she said aloud.

It was her spontaneous response to the breathtaking display. Nothing could beat nature for visual therapy. As she watched, the breeze gusted clouds of spent blossom to the ground, forming a deep crimson carpet.

She parked, as waves of uncomplicated delight rolled over her. She loved this place. North of Capricorn was another world, an artist's dream. There had always been an artist's colony here. Some of the country's finest artists had lived and painted here, turning out their glorious land- and seascapes, scenes of island life. Uncle Robert had a fine body of their work at the house, including a beautiful painting of the district's famous Poinciana Road that led directly to Moonglade Estate. From childhood, poincianas had great significance for her. Psychic balm to a child's wounded heart and spirit, she supposed.

Vivid memories clung to this part of the world. The Good. The Bad. The Ugly. Memories were like ghosts that appeared in the night and didn't disappear at sunrise as they should. She knew the distance between memory and what really happened could be vast. Lesser memories were susceptible to reconstruction over the years. It was the *worst* memories one remembered best. The worst became deeply embedded.

Her memories were perfectly clear. They set her on edge the rare times she allowed them to flare up. Over the years she had developed many strategies to maintain her equilibrium. Self-control was her striking success. It was a marvellous disguise. One she wore well.

A light, inoffensive beep of a car horn this time brought her out of her reverie. She glanced in the rear-vision mirror, lifting an apologetic hand to the woman driver in the car behind her. She moved off to the parking bays on either side of the main entrance. Her eyes as a matter of course took in the variety of tropical shrubs, frangipani, spectacular Hawaiian hibiscus, and the heavenly perfumed oleanders that had been planted the entire length of the perimeter and in front of the bays. Like the poincianas, their hectic blooming was unaffected by the powerful heat. Indeed the heat only served to produce more ravishing displays. The mingled scents permeated the heated air like incense, catching at the nose and throat.

Tropical blooming had hung over her childhood; hung over her heart. High summer: hibiscus, heartbreak. She kept all that buried. A glance at the dash told her it was two o'clock. She had made good time. Her choice of clothing, her usual classic gear, would have been just right in the city. Not here. For the tropics she should have been wearing simple clothes, loose, light cotton. She was plainly overdressed. No matter. Her dress sense, her acknowledged stylishness, was a form of protection. To her mind it was like drawing a velvet glove over shattered glass.

Auxiliary buildings lay to either side of the main structure. There was a large designated area for ambulances only. She pulled into the doctors' parking lot. She shouldn't have parked there, but she excused herself on the grounds there were several other vacant spots. The car that had been behind her had parked in the visitors' zone. The occupant was already out of her vehicle, heading towards the front doors at a run.

"Better get my skates on," the woman called, with a friendly wave to Mallory as she passed. Obviously she was late, and by the look of it expected to be hauled over the coals.

There were good patients. And terrible patients. Mallory had seen both. Swiftly she checked her face in the rearview mirror. Gold filigrees of hair were stuck to her cheeks. Deftly she brushed them back. She had good, thick hair that was carefully controlled. No casual ponytail but an updated knot as primly elegant as an Edwardian chignon. She didn't bother to lock the doors, but made her way directly into the modern two-storied building.

The interior was brightly lit, with a smell like fresh laundry and none of the depressing clinical smells and the long, echoing hallways of the vast, impersonal city hospitals. The walls of the long corridor were off-white and hung with paintings she guessed were by local artists. A couple of patients in dressing gowns were wandering down the corridor to her left, chatting away brightly, as if they were off to attend an in-hospital concert. To her right a young male doctor, white coat flying, clipboard in hand, zipped into a room as though he didn't have a second to lose.

There was a pretty, part-aboriginal young nurse stationed at reception. At one end of the counter was a large Oriental vase filled with beautiful white, pink-speckled Asian lilies. Mallory dipped her head to catch their sweet, spicy scent.

"I'm here to see a patient, Robert James," she said, smiling as she looked up.

"Certainly, Dr. James." Bright, cheerful, accommodating.

She was known. How?

An older woman with a brisk, no-nonsense air of authority, hurried towards reception. She too appeared pleased to see Mallory. Palm extended, she pointed off along the corridor. "Doctor Moorehouse is with Mr. James. You should be able to see him shortly, Dr. James. Would you like a cup of tea?"

Swiftly Mallory took note of the name tag. "A cup of tea would go down very nicely, Sister Arnold."

"I'll arrange it," said Sister. Their patient had a photograph of this young woman beside his bed. He invited everyone to take a look. *My beautiful niece, Mallory. Dr. Mallory James!*

Several minutes later, before she'd even sat down, Mallory saw one splendid-looking man stride up to reception. Six feet and over. Thoroughbred build. Early thirties. Thick head of crow-black hair. Clearly not one of the bit players in life.

Blaine!

The mere sight of him put her on high alert. Though it made perfect sense for him to be there, she felt her emotions start to bob up and down like a cork in a water barrel. For all her strategies, she had never mastered the knack of keeping focused with Blaine around. He knew her too well. That was the problem. He knew the number of times she had made a complete fool of herself. He knew all about her disastrous engagement. Her abysmal choice of a life partner. He had always judged her and found her wanting. Okay, they were friends, having known one another forever, but there were many downsides to their difficult, often stormy relationship. She might as well admit it. It was mostly her fault. So many times over the years she had been as difficult as she could be. It was a form of retaliation caused by a deep-seated grudge.

Blaine knew all about the years she had been under the care of Dr. Sarah Matthews, child psychologist and a leader in her field. The highly emotional, unstable years. He knew all about her dangerous habit of sleepwalking. Blaine knew far too much. Anyone would resent it. He wasn't a doctor, yet he knew her entire case history. For all that, Blaine was a man of considerable charisma. What was charisma anyway, she had often asked herself. Was one born with it or was it acquired over time? Did charismatic people provoke a sensual experience in everyone they met? She thought if they were like Blaine the answer had to be yes. One of Blaine's most attractive qualities was his blazing energy. It inspired confidence. Here was a man who could and did get things done.

Blaine was a big supporter of the hospital. He had property in all the key places. The Forrester family had made a fortune over the generations. They were descendants of George Herbert Forrester, an Englishman, already on his way to being rich before he left the colony of New South Wales to venture into the vast unknown territory which was to become the State of Queensland in 1859. For decades on end, the Forresters pretty well owned and ran the town. Their saving grace was that as employers they were very good to their workers, to the extent that everyone, right up to the present day, considered themselves part of one big happy Forrester family and acted accordingly.

She heard him speak to the nurse at reception. He had a compelling voice. It had a special quality to it. It exactly matched the man. She saw his aura. Her secret: She was able to see auras. Not of everyone. That would have been beyond anyone's ability to cope with. But *certain* people. Good and bad. She saw Blaine's now. The energy field that surrounded him was the familiar cobalt blue. She knew these auras were invisible to most people. She had no idea why she should see them, *feel* them, as *heat* waves. The gift, if it was one, hadn't been developed over the years. It had just always been there.

Once, to her everlasting inner cringe, she had confided her secret to Blaine. She was around fourteen at the time. There he was, so handsome, already making his mark, home from university. She remembered exactly where they were, lazing in the sun, down by Moonglade's lake. The moment she had stopped talking, he had propped himself up on his elbow, looking down at her with his extraordinary silver eyes.

> *"You're having me on!"*
> *"No, I swear."*
> *He burst out laughing. "Listen, kid. I'm cool with all your*

tall tales and celestial travels, but we both know auras don't
exist."
    "They do. They do exist."

Her rage and disappointment in him had known no bounds. She
had entrusted him with her precious secret and he, her childhood idol,
had laughed her to scorn. No wonder she had gone off like a fire-
cracker.

    "Don't you dare call me a liar, Blaine Forrester. I see
auras. I've seen your aura lots of times. Just because you
can't see them doesn't mean they're not there. You're nothing
but an insensitive, arrogant pig!"

He had made her *so* angry that even years later she still felt resid-
ual heat. She had wanted him to listen to her, to share. Instead he had
ridiculed her. It might have been that very moment their easy, affectionate relationship underwent a dramatic sea change. Blaine, the
friend she had so looked up to and trusted, had laughed at her. Called
her a kid. She *did* see auras, some strong, some dim. It had something
to do with her particular brain. One day, science would prove the
phenomenon. In the meantime she continued to see auras that lasted
maybe half a minute before they faded. Blaine-the-unbeliever's aura
was as she had told him all those years ago, a cobalt blue. Uncle
Robert's was pale green with a pinkish area over his heart. She
couldn't see her own aura. She had seen her dying mother's black
aura. Recognized what it meant. She had seen that black aura a number of times since.
    A moment more and Blaine was making his way to the waiting
room. Mercifully this one was empty, although Mallory could hear,
farther along the corridor, a woman's voice reading a familiar children's story accompanied by children's sweet laughter. How beautiful was the laughter of children, as musical as wind chimes.
    As Blaine reached the doorway she found herself standing up.
Why she did was beyond her. The pity of it was she felt the familiar,
involuntary flair of *excitement*. She was stuck with that, sadly. It
would never go away. She extended her hand, hoping her face wasn't
flushed. Hugs and air-kisses were long since out of the question between them. Yet, as usual, all her senses were on point. "Blaine."

"Mallory." He gave her a measured look, his fingers curling around hers. With a flush on her beautiful skin she looked radiant. Not that he was about to tell her. Mallory had no use whatever for compliments.

The mocking note in his voice wasn't lost on Mallory. She chose to ignore it. From long experience she was prepared for physical contact, yet as always she marvelled at the *charge*. It was pretty much like a mild electric shock. She had written it off as a case of static electricity. Physics. With his height, he made her willowy five feet eight seem petite. That gave him an extra advantage. His light grey eyes were in startling contrast to his hair and darkly tanned skin. Sculpted features and an air of sharp intelligence and natural authority made for an indelible impression. From long experience she knew Blaine sent women into orbit. It made her almost wish she was one of them. She believed the intensity of his gaze owed much to the luminosity of his eyes. Eyes like that would give anyone a jolt.

He gestured towards one of the long upholstered benches, as though telling her what to do. She *hated* that, as well. It was like he always knew the best course of action. She realized her reactions were childish, bred from long years of resenting him and his high-handed, taken-for-granted sense of superiority, but childish nevertheless. No one was perfect. He should have been kinder.

Blaine was fully aware of the war going on inside Mallory. He knew all about her anxieties, her complexities. He had first met her when she was seven, a pretty little girl with lovely manners. Mallory, the adult, was a woman to be reckoned with. Probably she would be formidable in old age. Right now, she was that odd combination of incredibly sexy and incredibly aloof. There was nothing even mildly flirtatious about her. Yet she possessed powers that he didn't understand. He wondered what would happen if she ever let those powers fly.

She was wearing a very stylish yellow jacket and skirt. City gear. Not a lot of women could get away with the colour. Her luxuriant dark gold hair was pulled back into some sort of knot. Her olive skin was flawless, her velvet-brown eyes set at a faint tilt. Mallory James was a beautiful woman, like her tragic mother before her. Brains and beauty had been bred into Mallory. Her academic brilliance had allowed her to take charge of her life. She had a PhD in child psychology. Close containment had become Mallory's way of avoiding transient sexual relationships and deep emotional involvement. Mallory made it very plain she was captain of her own ship.

The aftershock of their handshake was still running up Mallory's arm to her shoulder. She seized back control. She had spent years perfecting a cool façade. By now it was second nature. Only Blaine, to her disgust, had the power to disrupt her habitual poise. Yet there was something *real* between them; some deep empathy that inextricably tied them together. He to her, she to him. She was aware of the strange disconnect between their invariably charged conversations and a *different* communication she refused to investigate.

"I'm worried about Uncle Robert," she said briskly. She supposed he could have interpreted it as accusatory. "You told me it was a *mild* heart attack, Blaine. I thought he would be home by now. Yet he's still in hospital."

"He's in for observation, Mallory. No hurry." *Here we go again*, he thought.

"Anything else I should know?" She studied him coolly. The handsomeness, the glowing energy, the splendid physique.

"Ted will fill you in."

"So there's nothing you can tell me?" Her highly sensitive antennae were signalling there was more to come.

"Not really." His light eyes sparkled in the rays of sunlight that fell through the high windows.

"So why do I have this feeling you're keeping something from me?"

Blaine nearly groaned aloud. As usual she was spot-on, only he knew he had to work his way up to full disclosure. "Mallory, it's essential to Robb's recovery for you to be *here,* not in Brisbane. He's slowed down of recent times, but he never said there was anything to worry about. It now appears he has a heart condition. Angina."

"But he never told me." She showed her shock and dismay.

"Nor me. Obviously he didn't want it to be known."

Without thinking, she clutched his arm as if he might have some idea of walking away from her. He was wearing a short-sleeved cotton shirt, a blue-and-white check, with his jeans, so she met with suntanned, warm skin and hard muscle. She should have thought of that. Blaine had such physicality it made her stomach contract. He further rattled her by putting his hand on top of hers.

"You believe I have a moral obligation to look out for my uncle as he looked after me?"

"I'm not here to judge you, Mallory," he said smoothly.

"Never mind about that. I'm always under surveillance." Blaine had established the habit of meeting up with her whenever he was in Brisbane on business, which was often. His lawyers, accountants, stockbrokers, among others, were all stationed in the state capital. He made sure she could always be contacted. He was highly esteemed by her uncle, for whom he clearly stood in.

His hand dropped away first. It had made her uncomfortable feeling the strength of his arm and the warmth of his skin, but she wasn't about to waste time fretting about it.

"That's in *your* head, Mallory. It's not true. More like I've tried my hardest to be a good friend to you."

You difficult woman, you. He didn't need to say it; Mallory heard it loud and clear.

"Anyway, you're here now. You can give Robb your undivided attention for a few days."

"Whatever you say, Blaine. You're the boss." Heat was spreading through her. In the old days she had let it control her. Not now. As Doctor Mallory James, she was used to being treated with respect. "Uncle Robert and I are in constant touch, as you well know. Anyway, he has *you*," she tacked on sweetly. "Always ready to help. The figure of authority in the town."

"Do I detect a lick of jealousy?"

"Jealousy!" She gasped. "That's a charge and a half."

"Okay, make it sibling rivalry, even if we aren't siblings. You can't rule it out. I've known Robb all my life. My parents loved him. He was always welcome at our home. I remember the first time you turned up. A perfectly sweet little girl *in those days*, with long blond hair tied back with a wide blue ribbon. My father said later, 'Those two should be painted, Claudia and her beautiful little daughter.' "

"That never happened." A flush had warmed Mallory's skin. She wished she could dash it away.

"I noticed like everyone else how closely you resembled your mother," Blaine said more gently.

"Ah, the fatal resemblance! It was extraordinary and it impacted too many lives." She broke off at the sound of approaching footsteps. Sister Arnold was returning with tea.

Blaine moved to take the tray from her. "Thank you, Sister."

"Would you like a cup yourself, Mr. Forrester?"

How many times had Mallory heard just that worshipful tone?

Nothing would ever be too much trouble for Blaine Forrester; tea, coffee, scones, maybe a freshly baked muffin?

"I'm fine, thank you, Sister." He gave her a smile so attractive it could sell a woman into slavery.

"You could bring another cup, Sister, if you don't mind," said Mallory. There was really something about Blaine that was very dangerous to women.

"No trouble at all." Sister Arnold gave Blaine a look that even a blind woman would interpret as nonprofessional.

"I don't drink tea," Blaine mentioned as she bustled away.

"At this point, who cares? Sister likes bringing it. Makes her day."

He ignored the jibe as too trivial to warrant comment. "You drove all this way?"

She nodded. "One stop. It would have been a whole lot quicker to fly, but I don't enjoy air travel, as you know." She was borderline claustrophobic but halfway to conquering it.

"That's your Mercedes out front?"

"It is." She had worked long and hard to pay it off. "I love my car. You did *assure* me Uncle Robert was in no danger."

"With care and the right medication, Robb has many good years left in him."

"I hope so." Mallory released a fervent breath.

"Ah, here's Sister back with my tea."

"Don't forget to give her your dazzling smile."

"How odd you noticed," he said, his sparkling eyes full on hers.

An interlude followed, filled with the usual ping-pong of chat, largely saturated with sarcasm, most of it hers. Dr. Edward Moorehouse, looking like an Einstein incarnation with his white bush of hair and a walrus moustache, hurried into the waiting room. A highly regarded cardiac specialist, he possessed a sweetness of heart and an avuncular charm.

"Ah, Mallory, Blaine!" He saluted them, looking from one to the other with evident pleasure. His head was tilted to one side, much like a bird's, his dark eyes bright with more than a hint of mischief. "How lovely to see you together. I hear such good things about you, Mallory."

Mallory kissed him gently on both cheeks, feeling a sense of warmth and homecoming. "Doctor Sarah set my feet on my chosen path."

"Bless her."

Dr. Sarah Matthews had guided Mallory through her severe child-hood traumas: her terrible grief over the violent, sudden death of her adored mother, which she had witnessed, the later abandonment of her by her father, compounded by irrational feelings of guilt that she had lived when her beautiful mother had died.

"Wonderful woman, Sarah!" Moorehouse's voice was tinged with sadness. Sarah Matthews had died of lung cancer a couple of years previously, though she had never smoked a cigarette in her life. "We will always have a job for you if you ever come back to us, Mallory. No one has taken Sarah's place with the same degree of success. There are always cases needing attention, even here in this paradise."

She was aware of that. "Blaine tells me Uncle Robert has had a heart condition for some time. I didn't know that."

"Robb wouldn't have wanted to worry you." Moorehouse darted a glance at Blaine, then back to Mallory. "He has his medication. Robb is the most considerate man I know," he said in his soothing manner.

Mallory wasn't sidetracked. "He *should* have told me. I needed to know."

"Don't agitate yourself, Mallory. With care and keeping on his meds, Robb has some good years left to him."

"Some?" She had to weigh that answer very carefully.

"All being well." Ted Moorehouse spoke with a doctor's inbuilt caution. "You must be longing to see him. I'll take you to his room."

"I'll stay here." Blaine glanced at Mallory. "You'll want to see Robert on your own."

"I appreciate that, Blaine," she said gracefully. "Give us ten minutes and then come through."

They found Robert James sitting up in bed, propped up by pillows. An ecstatic smile lit his still handsome face the moment Mallory walked in the door. As a consequence, Mallory's vision started to cloud. Outside his room she had steeled herself, concerned at how he might look after his heart attack. Now his appearance reassured her. She felt like a little girl again, a bereaved child. Uncle Robert was the one who had been there for her, taking her in. She couldn't bear the thought of his leaving her.

The ones you love best, die.

She knew that better than anyone.

* * *

Robert James, gazing at the figure of his adored niece, felt wave after wave of joy bubbling up like a fountain inside his chest. She had come back to him. Claudia's daughter. His niece. His brother's child. His family. He was deeply conscious of how much he had missed Mallory these past years, although they kept in close touch. He had accepted her decision to flee the town where he had raised her. She had strong reasons, and he accepted them. Besides, clever young woman that she was, she had to find her place in the larger world. He was so proud of Mallory and her accomplishments. Proud he had been her mentor. His whole being, hitherto on a downward spiral, sparked up miraculously.

"Mallory, darling girl!" He held out his arms to gather her in. What he really felt like doing was getting out of bed and doing a little dance.

"Uncle Robert." Mallory swallowed hard on the lump in her throat. She wasn't about to cry in front of him, though she felt alarm at the lack of colour in his aura. Love for him consumed her. He looked on the gaunt side, but resplendent in stylish silk pyjamas. Robert James was elegant wherever he was, in hospital, in private. Like her father, he was a bit of a dandy. There were violet shadows under his eyes, hollows beneath his high cheekbones and at the base of his throat. But there was colour in his cheeks, even if it was most probably from excitement. He had lost much-needed weight, along with strength and vitality; hence his diminished aura.

"It's so wonderful to see you, sweetheart, but you didn't have to come all this way. Ted says I'm fine."

"You *are* fine, Robb," Ted Moorehouse said quietly. He knew how much his friend loved his niece. Her presence would do him a power of good. "I'll leave you two together. You can take Robb home around this time tomorrow, Mallory." He half turned at the door. "I expect you're staying for a day or two?"

Mallory tightened her hold on her uncle's thin hand, meeting his eyes. "Actually I've taken extended leave."

"Why that's wonderful, Mallory." Moorehouse beamed his approval. "Just what the doctor ordered." He lifted a benedictory hand as he headed out the door.

"Extended leave! I feel on top of the world already." Robert's fine dark eyes were brimming with an invalid's tears.

Mallory bowed her head humbly at her uncle's intense look of gratitude. It was *she* who had every reason to be grateful. She pulled up a chair and sat down at the bedside. Her touch featherlight, she smoothed his forehead with gentle fingertips, let them slide down over his thin cheek. "I'm so sorry if I've hurt you with my long absence, Uncle Robert. I know Blaine finds it so. He's outside, by the way."

"He's always there when you need him." Robert's voice was full of the usual pride and affection. "To be honest, I don't know what I would have done without him. He's been splendid, a real chip off the old block. Not that D'Arcy ever got to grow old."

Mallory bowed her head. She wasn't the only one who had lost a beloved parent. Blaine too had suffered. D'Arcy Forrester had been killed leading a cleanup party after a severe cyclone. He had trodden on fallen power lines that had been camouflaged by a pile of palm fronds. His passing had been greatly mourned in the town. The reins had been passed into Blaine's capable hands.

Robert James's hollowed-out gaze rested on his niece. "Does Nigel know about me?"

Mallory's smile barely wavered. "I've left messages. I'm sure he'll respond."

"I won't count on it." Robert spoke wryly. "Stripped of the mask of learnedness, my brother is not a caring man. What heart he had went with your mother. I would have liked to see him, all the same. We *are* blood."

Unease etched itself on Mallory's face. "Goodness, Uncle Robert, you're not dying." She tightened her grip as if to hold him forever. "You've got plenty more good years left to you. I'm here now. Father will be in contact, I'm sure." She was certain her father had received her messages. But her father hated confronting issues like illness and death.

Some minutes later, Blaine walked through the door, his eyes taking in the heartwarming sight of uncle and niece lovingly holding hands. "How goes it?"

"Wonderful, thank you, Blaine," Robert responded, eyes bright. "Ted says I can come home tomorrow."

"That's great news. I can pick you up in the Range Rover. To make it easy for Mallory, I can pick her up on the way."

So it was arranged, and they left the room.

She didn't so much walk as glide on those long, elegant legs, Blaine thought. Mallory moved like a dancer; every twist and turn, every smooth pivot. It was high time he dropped the bombshell and then stood well back for the fallout. He knew Robb hadn't told her. Robb simply wasn't up to it. It was part of Robb's avoidance program.

"Something I should tell you, Mallory." He hoped if she was going to shoot the messenger she aimed high.

"I *knew* there was something." Mallory came to an abrupt halt.

"Your psychic powers?" he suggested, that irritating quirk to his handsome mouth.

"Why don't you double up with laughter? What powers I have—which you *don't believe* is true—do work. I've been picking up vibes that something wasn't right. I can see by your face you'd prefer not to be having the upcoming conversation." Normally she spoke quietly. She was quiet with her movements as well. She never sought to draw attention to herself, but with Blaine her usually controlled manner became by comparison nearly theatrical.

"How right you are. I don't think you could guess, so I'll get right to it. Jason Cartwright has a job at Moonglade. On the farm."

The shock was so great she felt like ducking for cover.

Blaine showed his concern. "Hey, are you okay?"

For a moment she was too dumbfounded to reply. "Okay? I'm the expert on okay. I'm actually delirious with joy. Jason at the farm! What luck!" Her blood pressure was definitely soaring well above her usual spot-on 119/76.

He didn't relish this job, but he had promised Robb he would bring Mallory up to date. Robb tended to pull in the favours. "I'm sorry to spring it on you. Robb has never told you for his own reasons, but it's something you obviously need to know now you're here."

Take your time.

Stare into space for a minute.

She felt more like shouting, only that would be so utterly, utterly unlike Dr. Mallory James. "I love Uncle Robert dearly, but we both know he evades difficult issues like the plague. I *knew* he was keeping something from me."

"Your psychic powers didn't fill you in?"

"Oh, bugger off, Blaine." Abruptly she stalked off to her car, unlocking the doors with a press on the remote. She felt like driving back the way she came.

Blaine caught up with her with ease. "We can handle this, Mallory."

"*We?*" she huffed, rounding on him. "*We* will, will we? I love that. Your offer of support only grates."

"It's well meant. I've another surprise for you."

Her dark eyes flashed. "Don't hang about. Get it out. It's a bigger surprise than Jason working at the farm?"

For a woman who hated to lose her cool, Mallory's dark eyes gave Mallory, the enigma, away. They were *passionate* eyes. "He *runs* it," Blaine bit off. "No point in stretching things out."

She tried to find words. None came. "Well, he's had such a rotten time, he deserves a break," she said finally.

"I share your dismay."

"Then why didn't you stop it?" She was trying without success to dampen the burn inside her. "You can do *anything* when you want to. I've seen plenty of evidence of that over the years. You're the fixer. You run the town."

"I've never said that."

"You don't have to. Does the Queen tell everyone she's the Queen? She doesn't have to."

"Are you hearing yourself?" He too was firing up. "Be fair. It was Robb's decision, Mallory. It was never going to be mine. I couldn't take matters out of his hands. Robb owns Moonglade and the business. I've never been a fan of Jason's, but he's not a criminal."

"He *is* a criminal!" Mallory declared fiercely. "He betrayed me. He betrayed his family, Uncle Robert, even the town. That's criminal in my book. Honestly, Blaine, this is too much."

He agreed, but he wasn't about to stoke the flames. "I can't expect you to be happy about it. He's good at the job. He works hard."

Mallory shook her head. "The golden boy! That makes it okay for my married ex-fiancé to live and work on the doorstep? I suppose I can be grateful he wasn't invited to live in the house. Why couldn't Uncle Robert tell me himself? I don't give a damn how efficient Jason is. Uncle Robert—" She broke off in disgust. "It's the avoidance syndrome. It's rife among men." She propped herself against her car, in case she slid ignominiously to the ground. "Why does chaos follow me?"

"You're doing okay," he said briskly.

She waved off his comment. "What is *wrong* with Uncle Robb's thinking?"

"Obviously, it's different from yours."

"Ss-o?" she almost stuttered.

"If someone's decisions are different from our own, then we tend to assume it doesn't make a lot of sense."

"There's nothing wrong with my thinking, thank you." She became aware she was beating an angry tattoo on the concrete with the toe of her shoe. This wasn't like her. Not like her at all. Blaine found the terrible weak spot in her defences. "You didn't understand Uncle Robert's decision, did you?"

"The milk of human kindness? Blessed are the merciful, and all that?"

"I love the way you guys stick together."

"Oh, come off it, Mallory," he said, exasperated.

"We never know people, do we? Even the people closest to us. We always miss something. Uncle Robert needed to tell me. *You* of all people should know that."

"Damn it, Blaine, Jason's working at Moonglade is an outrage. It chills my heart. So don't stand there looking like business as usual."

He rubbed the back of his tanned neck. "It won't help to see it like that, Mallory. It's a done deal. You'd moved on. You didn't come back. It was well over six years ago."

"An astonishing amount of time. So you're saying *I'm* the one who is acting badly? Or am I an idiot for asking?"

"I don't think you're likely to hear the word 'idiot' in connection with you in a lifetime. Robb has a notoriously kind heart. He gave your ex-fiancé a job after it became apparent Harry Cartwright had disowned his only son. Robb is a very compassionate man."

"A sucker for a sob story, you mean. Okay, okay, *I* was a sob story. A seven-year-old kid who had lost her mother. A kid who was abandoned by her greatly admired, gutless father because I'm the spitting image of my mother. He couldn't look at me. I might have had two heads. I was his little daughter so much in need of a father's comfort, but my appearance totally alienated him. It was like I should have had plastic surgery, changed the colour of my hair, popped in baby-blue contact lenses. Ah, what the hell!" She broke off, ashamed of her rant.

"Mallory, I can't think of a single soul who didn't find your father's behaviour deplorable. You had a tough time, but you've come through with flying colours."

"An illusion I've managed to create."

"We all create illusions. I do get how you feel."

She raised her face to his, not bothering to hide her agitation. "How do you get it? Selma didn't run off from your wedding, so be grateful for that. Jason was an assassin. He stabbed me in the back, right on the eve of our wedding, remember? You should, you were there. You're *always* there, letting me know what a fool I am. Will you ever forget how the news of Kathy Burch's pregnancy spread like wildfire around the town? The disgrace. The humiliation. The shame. To make it worse, Uncle Robert had spent a fortune ensuring a fairy-tale wedding for me."

"I did warn you."

She felt the screws tighten. "Yeah, prescient old you! You must get great satisfaction out of knowing everything you said about Jason came true."

"He wasn't the most desirable candidate for your hand. Certainly not the husband of choice."

"Not your choice for me."

"Not Robb's choice either, even if he avoided saying so, which is a great pity, but seriously not worth getting into now. It didn't make me *happy* to say what I said then."

"I don't believe that for one moment. You relished the breakup. I was under so much stress, but you, superior old you, had to punch my stupidity home."

An answering heat of anger was rising in him. A certain amount of conflict with Mallory was par for the course. "How unfair can you get? If I'd told you I thought Jason Cartwright was absolutely *perfect*, you might have broken off the engagement."

She stared at him, wondering in consternation if he had spoken a truth. "There's always friction between us, isn't there?" she said, angrily puffing at a stray lock of her hair. "Bottled up forces."

"That's what *you* want, Mallory. Not me." Blaine stared down at her. Radiance had a way of playing around Mallory. The hot sun was picking out the gold strands in her hair and at her temples. The delicate bones of her face he found not only endearing but intensely erotic.

"Jason was kicked out of his home and the thriving family real estate business for reasons unknown. Was it money?" Mallory pondered. "Money causes big problems. Were the twins robbing their father on the side? Surely Uncle Robert pressed Jason for some explanation?"

"None forthcoming to this day." Blaine fixed a glance on her narrow, tapping foot.

She stopped the tapping. "You've always been able to get to the bottom of things."

"Wasn't my place, Mallory, as I said."

"Well, I can't accept you don't have *some* idea as to what the breakup was all about. You have your little network. All the businessmen in town want to hook up with you. They all know Harry. What about the grapevine?"

"Oddly, the breakup hasn't become the talk of the town. It's a mystery, destined to remain so."

She gave another dismissive wave of her hand. "I don't like mysteries, especially when they impact on my life. His parents doted on Jason. Could the fallout have been because of *me*? That would make me very uncomfortable indeed."

"I think not."

"How can you be so sure?"

"I know that much, Mallory."

She felt another quick surge of anger. "Of course you do, and a whole lot more you're not telling. Jason married Kathy Burch. They have a little girl."

"Her name is Ivy, a cute little kid. Kathy, however, is a very subdued young woman these days. Marriage and motherhood have—"

"Taken their toll?"

"The short answer is yes. Kathy is very much under Jessica's thumb."

She took a deep breath. Counted to ten. "A bigger bombshell is coming? Jessica is still on the scene?"

"Try to pry her away from her brother," Blaine said, his tone bone dry.

"Can no one kill her off? Or at least start looking into it?"

"No way of doing it without landing in jail," Blaine said laconically. "Those two were always joined at the hip. Jason and Kathy live in the old manager's bungalow, by the way. Robert remodeled it for them."

Mallory put her fingertips to her aching temples. "I didn't come prepared for these disclosures, Blaine. To think of all the phone calls, the e-mails, the visits, and never a word."

"Not so surprising, is it?"

She shook her head. "Not really. We both know Uncle Robert avoids unpleasantness. It's his problem area. As for *you*! You too left me completely in the dark."

"Mallory, I couldn't go over Robb's head."

"I had rights, didn't I?"

"You left, Mallory, telling us you were never coming back."

"Who would blame me? You're not the most compassionate man in the world, are you?"

"Compassion wasn't, still isn't, what you wanted," he said testily.

Mallory gave up. She would never win with Blaine. "I can't believe the Cartwrights would turn their backs on their only grandchild. Kathy might remain the outsider, but cutting off the little girl, the innocent victim, their own flesh and blood? The Marge Cartwright I remember was a nurturing woman."

"Maybe Jason is hitting back at his parents by not allowing them to see the child. She has a few problems apparently."

"Problems? What sort of problems?" Immediately Mallory started ticking off childhood disorders in her head.

"Health problems, and I believe she's a little wild. The whole town knows. Kathy is always at the hospital with her."

"How very worrying." Mallory's stance had softened considerably. "Is the child on medication? There are so many underlying reasons for behavioural problems. Sometimes it can be hard for a GP to differentiate. Kids are hyper for a wide range of reasons."

"I'm sure you're right, Doctor James."

Ah, the suavity of his tone! "Helping problematic children is my area, Blaine," she reminded him sharply. "I'd like to point out, while we're on the subject, I didn't allow bitterness over what happened to me and Jason to eat me away. What's past is past."

"Faulkner didn't see it that way."

"Okay, the past is never past. That way of yours of constantly having the last word drives me crazy."

"As I've suggested, it could be your bad case of 'sibling' rivalry. You were lucky you didn't marry Jason. He didn't break your heart."

"Did Selma break yours?"

He only shrugged. "Forget Selma. Look, I'm not in the mood for this, Mallory."

"Then you're welcome to go on your way. I'm not stopping you." She tilted her chin.

"Take a chill pill, why don't you."

She flared up. "Chill pill? I don't pop pills." She had been on antidepressants for some years. Occasionally she had panic attacks, but she worked to contain them without medication.

"Oh, for God's sake, Mallory! Why do you work so hard to misunderstand me? You're a psychologist. You know all about chill pills to control moods. I know this is difficult. If it helps, Cartwright is working hard. *Jessica* too."

For a split second she allowed her shoulders to droop. Then she straightened. No way was Blaine going to see her crumple. She'd do that when she was alone.

"Jessica Cartwright mightn't be a bucket of fun, but she's extremely competent," he went on. "She's far better than Jason at getting the best out of the staff."

"That's her big rap, is it? Jessica Cartwright gets the best out of the staff. Does she do it with a whip? Jessica was the nastiest kid in the school. She tormented the life out of Kathy Burch, when Kathy had suffered enough with that appalling father. Dare I ask how she wrangled the job?"

"Good question."

"With no good answer. Uncle Robert never liked her. He once called her a little monster."

"Tell me who did like her? Being pleasant never caught up with Jessica. She needed a job. The prospect of her finding work in town was uncertain at best."

"Most people had had kids in school with Jessica," Mallory said tartly.

"She mightn't have a winning personality, but Jason's life doesn't seem to be complete without her."

"Repressed development. Jessica is the alpha twin. She's always been in charge. But Jason is a married man now. If Jessica is around she probably spends her time ensuring every day is a real *bad* day for her sister-in-law. It's cruel for Jason to subject his wife to Jessica's TLC. God forbid he does it on purpose." Mallory felt up to her neck in unwelcome disclosures. "She's not his identical twin. They don't share identical genetic material. Jason was as pleasant as Jessica was downright nasty. Having said that, twinship is a deeply symbiotic relationship. I hope it's not too rude to ask, but what now? Is there a way out?"

"Not at the moment. Jessica lives in an apartment in town."

"I expect you own the complex?"

"I expect I do," he said.

"Modesty doesn't come in your size, does it?"

"If you say so, *dear* Mallory," he drawled. "To try to balance the good with the bad, Jessica has stuck by her brother."

"She'd stick with him if he were a total nutter. I really liked the Cartwrights."

"And they *loved* you." He went heavy on the *loved.*

"It was what it was," she said soberly. "So you got me here knowing all this?"

"I got you here for *Robert.* You owe him."

Memory after memory was sidling up. All of them full of angst. "I do so love you when you're righteous!"

"Me, righteous?" He spread his shapely hands.

"That's one of your big problems, Blaine. You're most righteous when you're in the wrong. And this is wrong."

"Would you have come back had you known?" He pinned her with his luminous eyes.

"So you deliberately kept me in the dark?"

"What would you have done had I told you the truth?"

She averted her gaze. "You don't know the workings of my mind, Blaine."

"You don't know mine, either."

"What's that supposed to mean?"

"You're smart. You'll figure it out. One piece of advice. Take it slowly."

She searched his face. Blaine was a central part of her life, but hunkering down inside her bolt hole had become a habit. "You make that sound like I could be steering into dangerous waters."

"And so you could be."

"They know I'm coming?"

Blaine nodded. "I expect they're feeling their own brand of trepidation. But life has moved on. *You* have moved on, Mallory. You're

Doctor James now, a highly regarded professional in your field. You could even be of help to the child."

The thought took the edge off her upset. "Only I'm certain Jason and his wife wouldn't want any help from me. Jessica was *never* my friend."

"I did tell you that as well."

"You did indeed." Between the heat and her sizzling emotions, she felt compelled to get away from him. "You know I've always thought you a complete—"

He cut her off, opening her car door. "No need to say it, Mallory. I can fill in the dots. And it wasn't *always*. Once we were good pals, until puberty got in the way."

"Puberty? Whose puberty?" she demanded, incensed.

"Why, yours, of course. I'm not a fool, Mallory. I know you hate it, but I know you too well."

"You'll need to do a lot of catch-up." With practised grace, she swivelled her long, elegant legs as she settled into the driver's seat. "You find this funny?" She caught the glint in his eyes.

"Not at all. I just hope you're relatively okay with it."

"Like I'm relatively okay with a Category Five cyclone. What time tomorrow?"

"Say eleven o'clock. Robert has a new housekeeper. Mrs. Rawlings. She lost her husband, Jeff, to cancer."

She nodded. "Uncle Robert did manage to tell me. I'm sorry. He told me plenty about your goings-on as well. We do so know he thinks of you as the son he never had. What did go wrong between you and Selma, anyway?" Her voice was edged with malice, when malice didn't come naturally to her. "I would have thought she was madly in love with you."

"You've managed to make that sound like one would have to wonder why."

"Just trying to spin your wheels. Besides, I didn't think you cared all that much what I thought."

"I'll let that one go as well. It was Selma who decided against an engagement," he offered with no loss of his iron-clad composure.

"It was the other way around, I fancy. She loved you, but you found you didn't love her, or not enough to get married. Had you a new conquest in mind?"

He made to close her door. "Let's swap stories at another time, shall we, Mallory?"

"Nothing in it for you, Blaine. I'm a closed book."

"Unknowable to everyone but *me*."

She could have cheerfully slapped him. Instead she found herself tightening her body against the odd tumbling inside her. "I assume that's your arrogance talking?"

"Not entirely. See you tomorrow."

He shut her door.

He walked away.

He didn't look back.

Her
AUSTRALIAN
HERO

MARGARET WAY

USA Today Bestselling author **Margaret Way** has written more than 130 books—many of them international bestsellers. She has been published in 114 countries and in 34 languages. Her novels are set in her beloved Australia, where she was born and lives to this day. Her stories always contain the beauty and rugged nature of rural and Outback Australia, as well as the rainforests and coral reefs of Northern Queensland.

44216411R00109

Made in the USA
Middletown, DE
31 May 2017

JUN 1 6 2017